VIRGINIA DARE
STORIES 1976-1981

FIELDING DAWSON

COVER & INTERIOR COLLAGES BY THE AUTHOR

BLACK SPARROW PRESS : SANTA BARBARA : 1985

VIRGINIA DARE: STORIES 1976–1981. Copyright © 1985 by Fielding Dawson.

ACKNOWLEDGEMENTS

Many of these stories first appeared in magazines in Scotland, England, Canada, Hong Kong, and the United States: *Bombay Gin, Boulder Monthly, Capilano Review, Imprint, New Letters, North Atlantic Review, ONE/4, Periodics, Red Hand Book, Rockbottom 5, Shankpainter, Words #10,* and *Writing*.

Special thanks to Terry Porter and Will Blais for the final issue (sad to say) of *The Falcon,* #19, which featured five stories.

LIBRARY OF CONGRESS CATALOGING IN PUBLICATION DATA

Dawson, Fielding, 1930–
    Virginia Dare : stories 1976–1981

    I. Title.
PS3554.A948V5   1985   813'.54   84-18573
ISBN 0-87685-618-0
ISBN 0-87685-617-2 (pbk.)
ISBN 0-87685-619-9 (signed)

For Mary and Edwin Reid

In memory of Gene

(1930-1956)

Then, drop by caustic drop, a perfect cry
Shall string some constant harmony, —
Relentless caper for all those who step
The legend of their youth into the noon.

> —Hart Crane
> *Legend*

Table of Contents

Author's Introduction

THE FIRST THREE of these stories were written in Vancouver, B.C., in the summer of 1976, while staying at Andrew Gruft's and Claudia Beck's Spanish Banks apartment — what a great view! which they let me have while away on vacation. My thanks are many.

Transitions! How to effect these keys to newness? In this book, in part, through visual images.* One title after another had increased to a point of mere print on white paper, and with Davenport in mind — I was making collages anyway — it clicked. Yet, rather than arranging a series of stories with images, both forms showed me the way toward a visual fiction in a surprising miracle of harmony. To paraphrase Stravinsky on the composition of music, I like to write more than writing itself.

The following three serve as post cards, thus the first six are prelude. At Dawn — the 7th title — just about appeared as a dream, which I embellished.

Voices begin.

I saw a potential centered lateral dialogue with quotes, rather than the standard from-the-left-margin approach. Testing, — to pass a football — in a lateral dialogue with narrative lines. Proven by ear, never at random. And, which came by ear, a test of a lateral new poetic dia-trialogue, each voice (unidentified) in quotes, identified by tone, brought to balance by narrative:

"Am I right?" "Maybe."
"I don't understand."
No wonder.

Worth considering, a trialogue of indecision:

"Am I right or am I wrong?" "Maybe both."
"I don't understand."
No wonder.

---

* The idea came from Guy Davenport. Note his sense — different than mine — of illustration as separate parallel development.

Four voices, tone true, thus identified. Note in both examples the syllabic brevity of "Maybe" and No wonder balancing through "understand."

* * *

Virginia Dare (do you know who she was?) declares the end of the *Penny Lane* series, and farewell to Blaze and pal Lucky, ah, how sad they are, but I must go my way. Thank you, dear friends. You were the foundation for this and future work — we'll meet again, one day. It has to be. But no, it won't be the same.

This book is my entrance into third person fiction, and open endings through transitions. The advent of fictional characters with points of view came as pure inspiration, arising from writing screenplays, the P.O.V. thunderbolt awakened sleeping alternatives. The last story, *You*, is a door to narrative anarchy, to undo the corset-concepts of beginning, middle and end, as well as lucid description and dialogue in 123 — ABC-type progressions, and the mistaken dogma that novelistic completion brings, or ties, all loose ends together. In a different, more organic, and human order, dialogue is vague, inarticulate, unspoken, progressions often unclear and often without apparent cause, thus loose ends form their own sequence and patterns, for flexible character rather than a rational and rigid plan. Loose ends form an unintended surface — the man in the dark blue suit who stutters. Loose ends put lines on people's faces. Loose ends are the essence of organic surface, a reason for human illusion and the baffling mystery in the mundane, which causes 'what happened' to tail away out of focus in the gleam of twinkling loose ends, those drifting snowflakes of connection.

Completion completes but its original potential in flow with what's learned and discovered along the way, causing it to change, therefore — so too the narrative will change, leaving, in its wake, reflections of vivid yet often irrelevant-seeming loose ends that refract and sustain initial creation.

This book draws to a close my involvement with the first person and autobiography, yet never to deny myself opportunities, for example to shed light, or set certain things straight — for the record, I will use that mode for that reason.

This work is accumulative and prismatic with the last page reflecting inward and outward, while the text, among other unusual processes, reveals three vanguard transitions radical to established form, thus casting new light on the adventure.

In all, this is of a dream begun in college, an innocent yet audacious reflection of Virginia Dare herself, and *Virginia Dare* in fiction, a mystery which, I pray, is compelling. An experiment beyond my fancy, never without it, determined that completion reflect if not mystify the beginning of the way out: these pages are the breakup of a former no-joke, diehard set of rules, and a breakthrough into necessary anarchy involving completion through unpredictable changes in a nontemporal composition of surprises, all unexplained, and *astonishing to me*, rather than that clocked plot used by writers working a hand-me-down formula that puts pages of dry ice in foil wraps, nylon tight. I say keep the pages open in arrangements across a structured narrative field sensitive to every influence, with the parallel and accumulative impact of its own change.

Good.

She opened the window, and stepped onto the fire escape, needle and thread in hand.

FD
Feb. 7, 1984
New York

11

VIRGINIA DARE

The Lady from South Africa
Bereft of Her Fortune

WESTWARD across the bay snow-capped Canadian Rockies rose against a long, low blue sky. Helen and Brian were drinking white wine at the table by her picture window. I was there too, drinking Russian vodka. Mark, Helen's oldest son, was being more than patient with us. It was around eight p.m., and we were due at the party. In fact we were late.

But she was telling Brian and me of her childhood on the big South African farm. Of the Zulu servant who smoked dope, and served suppers ever so slow, and of her parents who held hands at the table, and of her father who drank Scotch, loving it. Her voice was warm, deep, in memory. I know no one like her, save a dear, lifelong friend who spends her winters in Florida, and her summers in New Hampshire, fortune available.

And then there was me, who was broke.

Helen gave me a present.

A cardboard toilet paper tube. Near one end a hole about the size of a nickle had been cut, and over it a small square of aluminum foil had been taped with that opaque Scotchtape the editors at Random House use. But in the middle of the open foil, there was a slight indentation, and several pin punctures. This gift was because I had no pipe, where I was staying—downstairs in Andrew's and Claudia's place. Helen gave me a small block of hash, the size of the eraser on a brand new pencil.

A little overwhelmed, as I laughed she smiled and winked, and you have it on my authority: we smoked hash. Thus we went to the party, and in spite of all her dough being locked up in South Africa, she had her ways of loving and living, and they were legion. You therefore have it on my authority: she owned that wink.

15

Turning Wheel

1

I'M TYPING at the round table by the windows that look down the hill to the beach and English Bay, with downtown Vancouver and the mountains in the distance. Today is foggy—Friday, July 30th, whup there's the sun. That's Vancouver. Yesterday, while I wrote and watched three tugs move a flotilla of logs along the water, I missed my bluebottle fly. But not for long. He's back again, looking at the tip of my pencil, which isn't three inches from my typewriter. The slight tremble of my motions at the table doesn't bother him, nor does my typing.

A grey and white cat lives here too. White brush nose. I don't know his name, but he lives upstairs with Helen and the boys, and he reminds me of Sy—Enid and Michael Harlow's cat in New York. But this cat, in this house in Spanish Banks, has more than an apartment for his territory. He has three floors, a yard, and a long flight of steps down to the bush-lined street. He covers his turf like curiosity at home, along the roof or hallways, in and out from under eaves, drainpipes and into any room in the house through windows or doorways, down the steps out the front door and perhaps down to the street. It is all his neighborhood, and he walks, looks and listens like an inquiring but benevolent landlord. In the mornings while I typed, the cat often jumped up and dozed on the clean copy of the accumulating manuscript, in the sun by my machine, as if in a sense he wrote our story, so when I picked him up to slip a clean page of the manuscript under him, and then placed the carbon on the copy stack beside it, the cat was startled—not much, but a little—and he often rose, after I put him back down, and I stopped typing to watch. He crossed the table, stopped and looked at me as if to say "I get it" (his body told me, not his eyes), paused, hopped down onto the seat of the chair to my left, and thence to the floor. Helen says when he meows as he comes in, he's saying hello, and I witness wide and brilliant but empty eyes, which yet do seem questioning.

I leave the front door open, as well as the window across the apartment behind me, to get a cross breeze and cut the claustrophobia, as the place is so small, and the shelves and walls covered with plants, objects, books and things from around the world. So the cat comes and goes at will. It is, after all, his home, his territory, and his world.

The blue-bottle fly behaves likewise. And this creature, like the one that begins Chandler's *The Little Sister*, is a gorgeous husky I'm sure from the interior — Saskatchewan — and I somewhere recall that flies don't live more than a couple of days, but I have the feeling this fella's going to hang around a while. I never met a fly like this one, in the States or anywhere else, because the flies I've known often enjoy *me*, and what this bruiser likes is, without doubt, my literature.*

And, like the cat, the fly is right at home. Try that for some smoke. He's also curious. Like the cat. He walks around my table surveying my manuscripts, pencils, eraser, carbon paper, cigarettes, matches, coffee cup, etc., by following the edges of things *as they are arranged*. He takes a left turn at the bottom edge of the paper, walks the circle along the bottom of the coffee cup and follows the long straight line of the pencil, not more than a few inches from my right hand as I type, and a couple of days ago, when I first saw him, I stopped typing. I watched him walk around the eraser at the end of my pencil, cross the table, hop up and walk along the space bar, stop, and fly away, as maybe the texture was uninteresting — too smooth. And as well as corners, he likes the edges of things, which he crosses toward, as in walking across a field, the texture of the paper seems to please him, for he will stop, and stand staring down at the paper, as if deep in thought. Shuffles a little, body gleaming, transparent wings stilled. All this detail in what seems a writer's notion. Yes, it is true, my hands and fingers have handled the paper and pencil, and there is that human residue, but even so, two things — at least — are clear. First, I don't eat breakfast on this table. There's no food on it, and flies, including you me and the cats, can't live off paper. He walks around the bottom of the coffee cup, not the rim where my lips have been, with the invisible but available taste. Also, I have breakfast and lunch in the kitchen which isn't ten feet to my left and behind me, and there's a feast of dirty dishes in there, enough for all the flies west of Winnipeg, look — there he is again, just walked across the top of a manuscript, looked over the edge,

---

* Marlowe was a fool to have killed the fly. Had the detective realized he was getting a visit from his psyche (right there at the beginning — page one of *The Little Sister*), in lieu of what happened he would have made more conscious decisions, and through added psychic strength, been more in control of the end, into which he was drawn. When in doubt, ask the insect.

stepped off, walked across to the edge of the table and then flew away.

Second, which is incredible if not fantastic. He has never once landed on me. I'm wearing a short sleeved shirt, cutoffs, and am barefoot. It is mid-summer. I smell of sleep and food. Look! You won't believe it! He just landed on page two and walked along the typed sentence at the top of the page. I'm working on a new book, this is first draft, and the first two pages lie next to the carbon. I took a break from typing it to write about my remarkable fly. I've written about flies before — he who appears under the nose of a sleeping cat in *A Great Day for a Ballgame*, bears a resemblance to this fly, although he's a mere house-fly, but the most audacious I ever met.

New York flies drive me crazy. They're all over me — me, just up and had breakfast, and typing away, they love most of all my feet, ankles and legs, I often have to stop to brush them away or kill them. But this blue-bottle creature is different, and like the cat, comes and goes enjoying an obvious interest in things. Not as cool as the cat, instead almost frisky. When he goes, I'm going to miss him — I give him my sex because I identify with him. He's as close to my work as I am. Other blue-bottle flies have been here — their corpses adorn the windowsills, alongside shells of routine houseflies. There are other people, too — everywhere. But when this blue-bottle bigboy from Saskatchewan showed up, I realized it was a visit, and there he is again, snuffling around a stack of envelopes, turning, and crossing to and then stand-ing just beside the first draft of *Nancy Drew in Paradise*.*

He's following the curve of the table along the rim. Stops, and peers over the edge. Flutters his wings and rubs his feet together, takes a sun-shine bath a little like a cat, and then looks up.

Wings away into space.

2

I woke on Monday morning, August second — my forty-sixth birthday — to find, on a straight plumb line down from my typewriter, my blue-bottle fly on the floor, dead, with one wing gone. He was curled up, his back as green and shining as a child's Egypt. I picked him up and held him in my hand, gazing down upon him.

Most of all, I considered, how death would come on my birthday? Not an important birthday, like twenty-one, thirty, or fifty, but still, a birthday.

---

* Later, *Three Penny Lane*.

19

I had had human visitors the day before, and the day before that too, and sitting and talking someone made an attempt to kill my bright green fly, but I caught their hand, and stopped them (they thought I'd gone mad), I talked of him, and — smart guy! he was alert to it, or perhaps to me, for he showed them his stuff, and though they still thought I'd gone (you know), they did admit he was unusual. We watched him walking along the top edge of the clean copy, take a left and proceed up across to and then along the left edge of the first rough draft.

Maybe I don't know what it means, for once, and maybe he simply died in the stream of life just as I will, not to prove that we're all expendable or even that at least, none of us are eternal, and that death comes to flies as well as to writers, but perhaps to prove contact on an ever turning wheel. The rest — truth, and reality, involving facts, etc., him dying on my birthday is and are not, from this objective point of view, interesting, nor is the element of coincidence, which made me no more than self-conscious. But in a certain fluid connection to a certain corner of the galaxy, a form of life made contact with another, and that is more, much more than interesting.

What was a mere few days to the one, was to the other the span of his life without even knowing it. Thus something came to me and lived in full completion, and it was, then a message — perfect and natural that he would die on the day I would celebrate the day I was born, forty-six years ago, to tell me that in my own way I will swirl out into the universe following my own end, toward the desk of some phantom colossus at work in creation, who might notice me too, and upon completion, in whatever fashion, hold my poor corpse in his giant hand, and likewise gaze on me in wonder, as he considers his existence, the connection of all things, and the possibility of love and sadness in the full, roaring hurricane to oblivion, given immortality with one wing gone, in a few unhappy typewritten words on pieces of cheap paper, in a foreign city in a land away from home, by an alien and middle-aged man alone.

The Invisible Man

HEATHER, quite so. Exotic in a suburban sort of way with the standard caution, and the usual playing games with her brains. Her mask and her games were her cover — not altogether because she was from the provinces — but by that unspoken native innuendo, with her life thrust up against the Vancouver world, she let her glamor pave the way, while yet hiding in Grandma's living room, little Star Doll keeping her intellectual potential under the rug and using her wits to remind herself that what she selected was important regardless what anyone thought, much less the world and the chances it offered, which you know.

Care for a drink? John, make it two please. She had a sort of satisfaction in being in her place without quite being there, with her mask as the link. She was, in her own words, just plain her, which (apparent common sense) seemed, to her select friends, reasonable, and as they were feminine friends who admired their Heather, an odd ac/dc style circle formed around her, native in form as well as content if not in downright imitation of her, creating a little system of attractive bodies circling that Star, in the center of which she stayed, and oh yes she stayed as she was, struck by and stuck in reflected starlight. And as there was nothing between her and her circling bodies, so it seemed, they were just plain people, she threw away the connecting principle (space), and used her temporal wits to protect her ignorance, and her terror of new experience, creating a caution which, had she used her brains to realize it, blocked any kind of change at all, but as she had denied her potential for realization, she was free to do as she pleased, all the excitement of stealing cookies, although she was cool in this contemplation, thrilling her friends along the way, sitting beside me on the sofa at the party in West Van, cool as a teenage thief, and having picked up the paper edition of my newest book, looking at the cover and then at me she was as curious as a sleepy girl, asking, You wrote this?

I wrote it, I said.

She opened it and leafed through the pages folding the book back until she threatened to break the spine, just able to realize that the alien

21

object she held in her hands, which she was bending to breaking point, had been created by the alien man sitting next to her—asking her not to ruin his book, causing her to look surprised—she closed the book and put it on the cushion between us. The cover and first few pages had curled back. I remarked upon that. She smiled it was okay, she hadn't hurt it that bad. I pointed at it and said no? Cover and pages curled? Don't you know about books? "That's a book," I said, "my book," my thumb on my chest: "I wrote it."

She was hurt, gave me big eyes mixed in a dense north woods look—what had she done?

I'd known teenage kids in Brooklyn who read the headlines of *The New York Daily News* as if there were eighteen inches between the words and the paper. They too had the north woods look. So I looked at her the way you look at the north woods, they do not change in the seeing, but her eyes brightened, and from a dense yet simplistic associational process the word book became *book*, and she said, having no idea how near-beautiful she was in her innocence, nor how seductive in her ignorance—a strange but not uncommon phenomenon in Vancouver—she mentioned, and began speaking, with considerable intent, of Jack London, causing me to remember a young woman I'd met in college who had read one book—just one, so there was a four thousand mile, twenty-five year curiosity I was covering, realizing two women had gotten so far with so little effort. I had difficulty listening. John, these drinks are delicious, thanks, and keep that ace for yourself. It wasn't long after Pearl Harbor I became interested in contemporary writers, for instance, Saroyan, *My Name is Aram*—yes, Saroyan—you too? Also Olson, and as he wrote me, so too Robert Duncan, but looking at Heather, she was, I thought, about twenty three or four, although she looked older, for her face was lined, with a shade of sienna under her eyes, and her skin seemed tough, effect of neglected potential, playing games, yet her bright, warm dark eyes had a youthful arrogance and candor which impressed me, and warmed more indeed than my heart. You know me, me and how things seem. She was thirty, and I was shocked.

Do you mean, I said, that you have come all this way, from zip to thirty, and this is all you have?

She asked what I meant as Susan and I finished our martinis. You must be kidding, I said. John? when you get a chance, two more please, which Heather rejected, so I asked, You don't know what I mean? I mean it, I said. Is that it?

She blinked, looked away and then back, smiled, fiddled with the

22

stem of a glass of Australian white wine and said she thought so, then, yes she said. Yes, I don't know what you mean, so I said Do you mean that you have come all this way, from zip to thirty, and this is all you have?

What's all?

I said, Jack London.

The newspapers, she said. "Swell," I quoted. I don't know much about art, she said. That's the best place to begin, said I.

I want to read, she frowned, in part sucking as well as chewing on her thumb, what Australian wine does for you, I tossed off my vodka.

John Reynolds, Susan says, you're wonderful. He's the best bartender in Canada, and with Frank in New York, number two on the continent. We sip icy fresh drinks. I look across English Bay at Heather. Flat lips, wide mouth, like Jeanne Moreau with rather deep bracketing lines meaning, perhaps, that she did talk, but not to me, and in deliberate naiveté her silence was forced beyond her comprehension, so I had to wait while she figured out what she was thinking about, in company with a hundred million television viewers, terrified of anything new, their attention span lasting until the commerical.

Read what you like, I said.

Where do I start? she asked. I don't — know what I like.

Start anywhere. Let books come to you.

She became irritated, angry at all this, but as anger involved a response to an experience she was sorry to have gotten into (being angry at me), and in fear of speaking the anger, she began circling around a way to meet the problem in that certain way she could select, but because she hadn't yet used her intelligence in this form she was threatened by the release of an unused potential — how she did feel about this bullying bastard from New York who was upsetting her, and on top of that — was himself angry at her!

Don't let anybody tell you what to read — ever (thinking of Virginia Woolf's essay). If you like newspapers, read books by journalists. They're often good, and — otherwise, if a book catches your eye, try it.

She gave me a suspicious look. She was just plain people. Who had treated her like this?

Books talk, I said. If you give them a chance, they'll tell you things.

She nodded. They do live, she said.

I grinned. Our eyes held. She smiled. God! How *beautiful!* Long black curls and a red kerchief around her neck, her whole lush body in black and tan cotton and leather plus buttons, snaps, strings, a kind of Arkansas lady gone north in the Sixties, drifted west, over the Rockies via

Burnaby ended up in Vancouver – West Vancouver at that, a trip for sure, but not quite, it seemed, complete, – did it matter? I drank a new drink and she sipped that Kangaroo gasoline while I listened to her generalize, in numb little loops, how she loved books, interesting people, and Life.

I agreed on the Life aspect, rather than the other two, and as I was wondering if I should tell her why, she amazed me.

I hate ignorance, she said.

The enemy, I responded, almost beside myself – but, then I wondered if she hated herself (ignorance – she probably did), and I rather hated myself, for these thoughts, but gave her a look which said tell me more. She blushed, got angry, turned aggressive.

You think I'm ignorant, don't you?

I think you're a fool, I said. If you imagine this life you're living, with those simple-minded copycats around you, is what the Life you say you love is, try using the brains God gave you.

She pursed her lips, sipped petrol, and lowered her head.

You're right, she said.

The message is, not me. You've resisted for thirty years, and the longer you continue, the tougher living is going to be, and as you proceed you'll end up your own worst enemy, hating that circle that surrounds you but defending it – and needing it – because you created it.

She looked at me.

Circle?

Those so-called friends of yours, whom you allow to stimulate you while they emulate you. Do you think they're worth you?

"Stop," the voice said, and I did, remembering the innocent, latent, ignored, suppressed and repressed virgin potential I've witnessed everywhere I've travelled, in good natured, well meaning people, most of whom couldn't help it. But there were a precious few who could help it, and they never failed to anger me. A truth I couldn't help.

I know you're angry at me, I said, but I'm angry at you, too, because –

I'm not angry at you, she interrupted.

Oh yeah? Maybe not up top – I was getting angrier – but at bottom you are. I can see it. Plain as day. Tell me you resent me. I'm angry at you, and I'm intruding – you almost broke my book, and my book is me.

You can see me?

She was afraid of that, but curious, ah, ha ha ha.

As through glass, I said. Paused. Look here, I said, try and understand that I'm angry because I've seen too much brilliance, talent, beauty and even genius wasted behind the determined defense in the face of something new or different.

Do you think I'm brilliant? (enthusiastic) Or talented? (she pouted) I'm not.

Heather, I said — added:

How do you know?

Well, she answered, or tried to, raising her shoulders and inhaling quick, dark eyes on mine, and — and then, in her quarterback switch-away, habitformed to miss it, she forgot her answer, stammered the lie that she was aware of what I meant, and in a little step-away dance, almost coldly, said yes, it was true, she was angry at herself.

And? I asked, knowing it was easier for her to be angry at herself than at someone else (me) — while sidestepping the issue.

I don't know, she said, and fell silent. Pause. I'm not used to this, she murmured, sipping that Down Under juice, mind running around its familiar silent circle. But then, it was true. She didn't know. She didn't know how to begin a thought unless it contained its own conclusion. Continuity unknown. Simple. I asked, in hope of coming back to it —

Why are you angry at yourself?

She scowled as if angry, but her face showed conflict, she was being seen, played some games — said,

I don't know, but there are — are so many things in life that I —

Ah, I could have waited as well as danced all night, while she again generalized in circles, and again claimed refusal of new experience, and I knew what she would have to give up to achieve what she didn't know, nor could anticipate knowing.

Desire, I said, has a continuity of its own, in the lucid pointblank fact of itself wanting other things — places, persons, which takes us, if we dare, beyond what we are and were, toward a fresh new passionate self that knows, yet will never know, but must ever lust to learn.

I have to go, she said, gazing at the small machine on her wrist. It's getting late.

It was never so early, I countered. If you lose me, you lose a chance.

Tell her!

Don't lose me, I said. You're too real. I see it.

It's well after one, she said, and I have to go, and she rose from the sofa into her usual self, stood in her color and little Star flame on her feet in her North American skin and clothes, face shut, courteous, objective, offering to drive me home in the full vision of an anger or rage

25

that should have left me in bloody chunks all round English Bay, small talk all the way, in her car, except at the end, John, here's to you, when I invited her up to witness the view — that wonderful view from across the Bay, like a sweet old sentimental passion-song, but superlatives were undesired things by then, and Heather declined.

Come on, I said, ever wanting — come on inside with me. We can look across and see Vancouver —

"I live in Vancouver," she said, not watching as I got out of the car, closed the door, and walked up the steps in darkness hearing her drive away.

Alice Is Floating Around

OH, SHE'S GREAT, Debora said on the phone. She's five and a half pounds, eighteen inches long, dark hair, dark eyes, red lips, a John Daley nose, long fingers, long toes. It was an extraordinary delivery. Doctor and midwife were great.

"What's her name?" I asked. Tuesday, May 24, 1977.

The Man Who Was Thirsty

STANDING DOWN the bar.

Plump bald, bushy red hair on the nape of his neck, skin the color of a banana. Gummy mouth, toffee buckteeth, no eyebrows wraparound dark glasses transparent ears, blue, scarlet-veined nose. No chin hollow down a thick stump neck, tits chest in a stained, open, dirty white shirt, mottled, rumpled red and green plaid jacket, gray flannel pants too tight hiked up, white silk socks with yellow circles sagging on aspirin-colored ankles tiny feet in oversized ripped black leather shoes FBI hat on the bar at his elbow as he drank gin and Seven-Up no ice, flat draft beer chaser, smoked a menthol filter king to the filter inhaling nothing exhaling less coughed, stared at the dead smoke in skeletal no-knuckle fingers, dropped the butt on the floor, scratched his nose, and sighed.

More Bartok

LITTLE THINGS drive me crazy. Yeah, well this one, I *had* to do something about — about what? I'm telling you! The floor of my loft, you know, unh huh, is big so I use an industrial dust mop — it's about two feet wide — and a few months ago, months? Yep, I noticed that the nut on the bolt that goes through the mop's metal sleeve and then through the base of the wooden handle, where the handle joins the mop — the nut was missing, so the mop-end mechanism was loose and squeaky and I couldn't shake the mop out because of that loose bolt, the mop might fall off, so I've been careful, seeing to it that the bolt was as secure as it could be, made little piles of dust on the floor I later swept up with a brush and dust pan, whereas before I'd shaken the mop out the back window, got it? Yeah. Okay, so the other day I took the bolt out and to remind me to get a new nut, I put the bolt in my pocket, the front right hand pocket where I keep my keys, okay? Yeah. I managed to spin around town for a week with that bolt in my pocket, remembering it too late when the hardware stores were closed, etc., sure, figuring (more and more pissed off at myself), if I could complete this project I could do anything, find the lost chord — got that? Yeah. Yeah the mystery of life, right, so, one bright blue flash day I went around the corner into my neighborhood hardware store and said to the guy — they're nice guys — me a little self-conscious — You? Sure, will you listen? All ears! Okay, I said — to the salesman — Listen John, in my ten years of selling retail and wholesale I got to know a pain in the ass when I saw one, so I'm telling you you're looking at a pain in the ass and he laughed.

I don't mind, he said. Don't worry about it. What's the problem?

I took the bolt out of my pocket and showed it to him saying I need a nut for this.

He took the bolt, looked at it, walked to the shelves behind the sales desk, took down a small box, opened it, took out a nut, and we both watched the nut not going on. He put the nut back in the box, put the box back on the shelf, took down another box, and we watched as he tried again and said We don't have a nut for this bolt, so he took down another box, opened it, and gave me a new bolt with a new nut on it and said try this which, to make a not real awful long story shorter, I did when I got home and it was perfect. A couple of days later I went back and thanked him.

But before, in the store with John, it seemed that the circumference of the bolt was too small, and would be loose, even with the new nut, but I left with it anyway, stood on the corner—southeast corner on Park South (you know) (yeah), the new nut and bolt in my hand I kept thinking maybe I should go in and tell John it seems too narrow, but a voice, a voice spoke into my ear, saying—"Look, go to the bar, have a couple of drinks and think about it. If it doesn't fit, take it back. John'll give you another one," which I did. I followed my voice and—

Well, that makes sense. What'd he charge you?

I asked him! How much—

Two cents, John said *two cents?* Yeah! Two cents!

Jesus. Does the mop work?

Better than ever. I oiled it. Not a squeak. Right? Hey. Right. Let's have another.

At Dawn

AT DAWN, in a town called Am-timan, quite a ways south of the Sahara Desert, a man sat up in his bed —

"What a strange dream I had!"

His wife, whom he had awakened, sat up beside him. They looked at each other.

"I just had the most strangest dream!" he exclaimed, and looked across the room, out the window. With her.

The sun peeped over the trees.

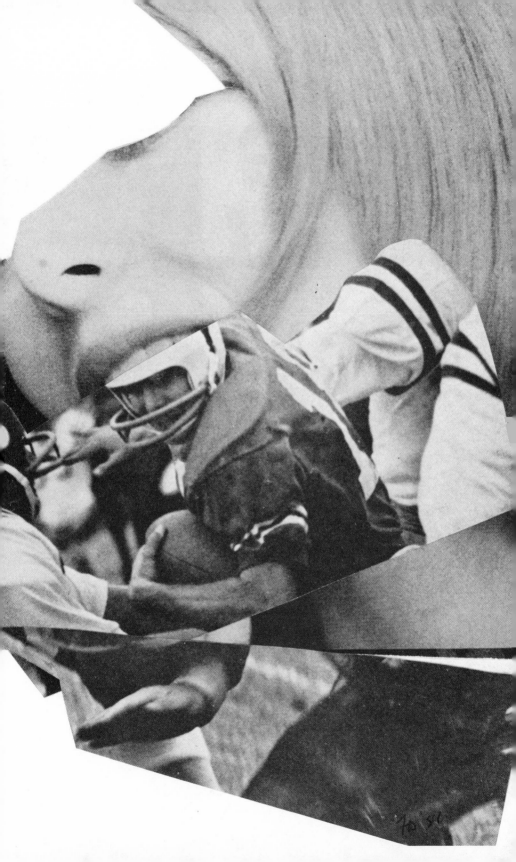

Virginia Dare

VIRGINIA DARE was reading at the
kitchen table, unaware of the neighbor's Chrysler in the driveway. The
front door closed. He came in.

A tall thin man stood beside a short
squat guy in front of the candy stand
in the lobby of the post office. A
blind man stood behind the counter,
listening.

"I saw a good movie on tv last night."
"I must have missed it," said the blind man. "No, hey — no, I meant — "
"What was it about?" asked the blind man. "Reading?" "A guy who had
a — " "Dog," the squat man, the dog ate spaghetti. "Yes." "Aw," the other.
"C'mon. You remember." *The Lido.* "Yeah." With salt and pepper. "So?"
"A novel." "*So!* So *what!* Am I a fuckin' dummy?" "Would you like a
Coke?" "No." "It was about a movie!" "A movie!" (the blind man) "A
movie about a movie?" "Carlton Heston!" "Which fuckin' *movie*, I
mean." "Thanks."

"Carlton Heston in Egypt, they get the castle, he gets killed."

"Is it good?" "Thought you said it was about a movie." "Maybe I was
wrong. I thought I thought it was — " The vet was amazed. "Yes." "Maybe
you get confused." "Yeah. Maybe." "What happened to the dog?" asked the blind man. "He's in L.A." "You guys." "How do you know?" —
the blind man. "He wrote me." "What did he say?" "Bow wow." A
woman in a tight red dress, dark glasses and green paint on her fingernails walked by and there was a lull in the conversation. The blind man
was enjoying himself. "What else did he say?" "The curry was too hot."
"Curry?" "Curry." "They don't have curry in Egypt." "Sure they do. At
dawn, in the kitchen in the castle. It kills hangovers." The blind man
laughed. The tall guy said they didn't have castles in Egypt, "they have
those, — you know, those . . . castles are in England." "Japan, too," said
the squat guy, "but you said he was killed in a castle. Carlton." "A fort."

37

"That's different," said the blind man, as a shadow crossed marble in a voice difficult to make out. The blind man gave over a Mars, bar: shadow paid floating away unwrapping. "I never saw a fort," said the blind man. "What do they look like?" "Square." Squat guy. "Big." Tall guy. "Do they have rooms?" Blind guy. "Lots." Who is there. "It depends." The blind man sensed the distraction and fell, silent on the edge of a plain very tall indeed, spear in hand with a gesture as soft as a caress he parted thick undergrowth, just a little, bent closer, and looked in, what he saw made his eyes bright and brought a smile to his lips, for a lion, fifty yards beyond, was sound asleep and dreaming. The warrior whispered.

"He is dreaming of me."

Depressed, in thoughts of the Game Warden, who also dreamed of him.

"Maybe."

She thought.

Although not much given to thought, and in this she was as ordinary as her husband and the house next door. Yet in a varying affection as autumn and high school football running through the center of town: a line drawing of a young man who died in a Navy search plane that exploded mid air at night in the Bermuda Triangle — There's a story! What do the people say? He went out in the rain and stood on his lawn, while she watched through the window for another in the rain until, aware of her reflection in the glass, and other than the man on the television set talking to her, himself being watched, there was no sound, she turned away and resumed reading.

What did he do?

He came in from the beach, and after drying himself, went to her, and held both her hands in his.

She laughed, in the still damp of him, that the top of the mountain had been leveled for a new airport, mattered not, and though weeds ran down the hills into the ocean they slept in the valley with the secret, almost blank expressions of humans who don't know how to read but do anyway, and after having seen a tv program they were supposed to like and in fact did, went out for hamburgers. In a sense they had it figured out, it wasn't so much that the thrill was gone, unh unh, the thrill was there, and to be taken into account, like kids growing up.

They would.

The talk was of oil and basketball, baseball, earthquakes, breakfast, catfood, supper, tv and silver when Hugh visited. But Hugh stayed.

38

Nice kid. Her sister's oldest boy, and when in a word he didn't fit in back there was the why-in-the-world? answer he left — home, the city and almost his country! Had everybody given up on him? Anyway, she began to care — she didn't know it, he looked like her.

If things had been different — if he wasn't so powerful in body, he might look, or appear, even seem like a girl — a woman, he sure was sexy, and as he had what was evident but — *like* them. It was so — beyond her, as in a spun story, what will it tell? He was the first string quarterback on the new season's team and he went away leaving everybody baffled, well, she thought — but there it is again. And after the last war, — she looked out the window at the weeds going into the ocean, and seeming quite large, a seaplane banked over her house and headed south to complete the novel, sky so blue it hurt her eyes. Did she love him? Perhaps. Or was it her? The conjecture hung, like a long look in a mirror fading in the echo of the plane.

Ghost Riders in the Sky

"WHAT ARE YOU DOING?" she asked. Holding a broom and looking down at him. He lay on the sofa. Eyes closed.

"I'm worrying about the world," he replied.

"You said you were going to call David."

"I'll wash them myself."

"Do you know how many windows there are?"

"Thirty eight."

"Why are you worrying about the world?"

He opened his eyes, sat up, and looked at her. "Because," he said, "the world is in bad shape."

"If you did the things you had to do, you wouldn't worry about the world. The world will take care of itself."

"I can't help it. I'm a worrywart."

She sat cross-legged on the floor with the broom across her lap, and looked up at him, as he looked down at her. The sun came through the window and lay in her lap. An orange cat came into the room, and curled up in the sun.

"I know why you're worried," she said.

"Why."

"Because you're nervous."

"That's true."

"I also know why you're nervous."

"Good."

"We'll see. It's only for a week. You'll be back."

"Nuts."

"It isn't so bad."

"That's what you say."

"That's what you should say."

The telephone rang.

"You get it," he said.

"No, you get it. It's for you."

"I know," he said, rising, and going into the hallway, he picked up

41

the receiver.

She heard him talking, and realized his flight had been changed. He came back into the room, sat on the sofa and lit a cigarette. She sat beside him.

"I have to catch the three-twenty flight. Know what that means?"

"Jesus," she said.

"Yeah. Want a beer?"

"Sure."

He went into the kitchen, a sunny place, but then the whole house was sunny, there was a lot of space, and he opened two cans of Bud and returned to her. They drank beer. She envisioned him landing in L.A. in the rush hour, and frowned.

"I have to call Woody," he said.

She nodded. "What a drag."

"Yeah, it is."

But he called Woody and told him, which turned out better. The story conference had been postponed.

"Why in hell didn't you call me?" he said to Woody.

"I just found out," Woody said. "Funny, isn't it?"

"Funny?"

"Yeah. F as in fuck, u as in —"

"You."

Woody laughed.

"See you." Click.

"How's Woody?" she asked. She was sweeping the floor.

"Funny. Nip?"

"No thanks. Yes. Sure."

He filled two shot-glasses with vodka, they drank them down, used beer for the chaser, had two more shots, and that afternoon he began washing the windows. The next afternoon he flew to Los Angeles, and a week later he was back.

"How'd it go?" she asked, glad to see him. He grinned.

"Wonderful," he laughed, went to the telephone, tore it off the wall, ripped the cord free, took it outside and threw it in the lake, came back, kissed her, said,

"It was terrific."

She asked: pointing at the lake, "What was that about?"

"Woody."

He made two vodka tonics, and taking a blanket they went outside and lay on the blanket on the grass.

Nice view.

"What happened?" she asked.

He sipped his drink. He made good drinks. He sighed, and looked at the sky.

"I'll tell you," he said, "but there's no end to it. I mean, things are still going on."

"But I thought you were going to finish it! Isn't that what Woody said?"

"That's what Woody said, but what Woody says is very very different from what Woody does!"

"That's true. What happened?"

He told her. She couldn't stop laughing.

"You know his next move!"

"You bet I do."

True enough. The next afternoon Woody came bouncing up the road in a blue Hertz, parked by the lake, and walked across the grass to where they were sitting, plucking a chicken.

"Hi," Woody said.

They said hi.

"I have to talk to you," Woody said.

He did. Nothing new. Woody stayed for supper, they got pretty drunk, Woody spent the night and the next day the two men drove in Woody's blue Hertz, to the airport. What happened? He came back. She became pregnant, they got married, the play was a flop, and Woody, on an assignment for Newsweek went to Hong Kong, fell in love with a beautiful teenage Eurasian girl, and — got married? No. No? No. Fade out.

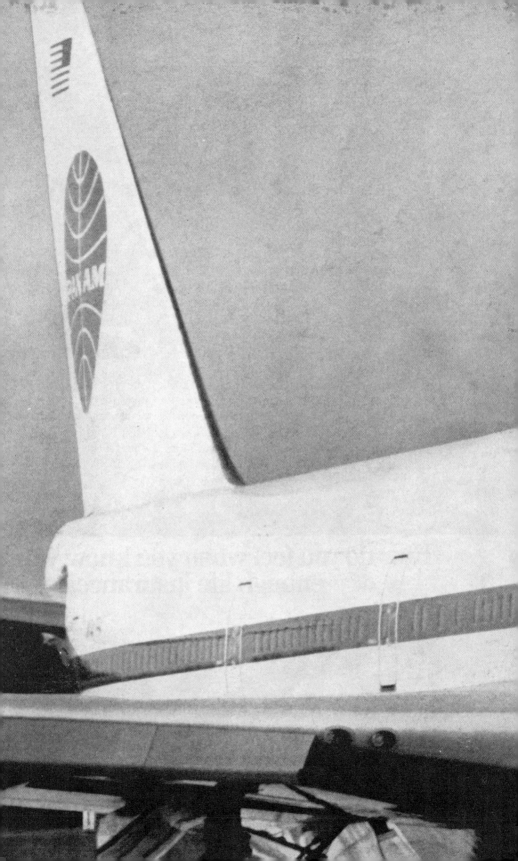

The Blue Lamp

"WHAT WOULD YOU SAY if the telephone rang?"
She smirked.
Hello. Are you asking? Her expression said no.
She smiled.
"Is it for you?"
"Look here," he said. "There's a fellow out by the pool, says he's a reporter."
"I *thought* so," she snarled, rising from the red sofa, *"I told you to tell Junior to keep those pulp bastards away from here!"*

Special Delivery

DOWN THREE STEPS into the store. In mind, the articles in the bag in hand: six bright colored crewel embroidered tote bags, six colorful plain bags, eighteen silk scarves and three dozen inlaid turquoise bangles. He checked to make sure he had his order pad and pen, which he did, and walking along the aisle between rows of retail objects, he approached the handsome waxen professional male doll who was, on the q.t., a salesman. On the upper east side they are in legion.

The store, as if made for him, the whole store, from front to back, was narrow, and white, even the floor, the ceiling, to form a white enamel boxlike room in the shape of a T, opening out on the right and left in the rear, where there was a small, delicate white iron and formica restaurant. Little tables, little chairs. Ice cream. Cookies.

But up front, in the store part of the store, above white octagonal-shaped floor tiles, the shelves were white. The counters, an occasional chair, a table or two, were white, and spotless, not a speck anywhere, overhead, set into the ceiling, a white ventilator, the inside of which was white. The cash registers were white, on the white wall behind which gleamed six white antique pitchers on a white shelf.

But in the objects for sale, color abounded, yet the contrast was so severe the effect was rather than determined neatness, a desperate, *furious* order. All the bright, cute little things, each in an almost forced arrangement to catch the eye. Cute little salt and pepper shakers, little Shirley Temple pitchers, fancy match boxes, wicker chairs and stools, games and toys of all kinds, expensive and not so expensive jewelry, round and square, colored and chrome mirrors, (real) dolls, Charlie Chaplin canes between mirrors the blue of post war Dresden in memories of childhood above rugs with Andy's Marilyn on them, cardboard Garbo fans beside Garbo hats, above and alongside useful boxes, and boxes inside boxes of all colors, nestled in, enamel smooth, as well as crystal and clean quart, pint and half pint Mason jars with the wire spring locks, each filled with all kinds of candy and gum. Soap for every use, towels and washcloths, boxes of stationery, and round plastic

47

boxes of nuts, and all sizes and varieties of imported chocolate. Color-ful Indian jewelry, Madras throws, shawls from Mexico, puzzles from Germany. Cocoa from Switzerland. Boxes of real Italian spaghetti. And more. A lot more. In the restaurant section sweet fresh New Jersey farm butter, French bread flown in that morning from Paris. Home made chile. Foot long hotdogs. And more. Much more. But action —

A fellow who resembled the doll-like gentleman but who appeared to be the manager, or one of them, had joined the salesman at the counter — and they were paying attention to a customer, a tall, nar-row, painted graycoated furlined flippy middle-aged woman wiggling her grey gloved fingers while speaking superlatives to a miniature glass poodle in hand at arm's length.

The fellow who had just entered the store, name? Red. Okay? Sure. Moved closer, for it was the manager he wanted to see, for he had some things to sell him, but the manager and the salesman smiled to the woman, and the salesman inquired did she want it giftwrapped? Oh dear yes.

The manager glanced at Red, said, "Just one moment, sir," and as he filled out the woman's receipt, the salesman wrapped her present in fuchsia tissue and put it in a little chartreuse box, fingers dancing.

The manager went behind the counter, and ducked out of sight, look-ing through the shelves below. The salesman handed the lady the boxed glass poodle, but the woman, it seemed, remembered something she had forgotten, put the box and receipt on the counter, pivoted to her right, and seeing Red, tore off her coat, bunched it in her hands, and while the salesman gaped, Red stared, she was going away, on a sharp angle from an original intention she couldn't recall, she beat her face with coat-encumbered fists, swung her head from side to side, dropped her coat on the floor, and as her hands fell to her side, she gazed with no expression over Red's shoulder and out the front window. Face blank, she then spoke. On the upper east side, they are in legion.

"I'm all right. It's just a little cough."

She picked up her coat and put it on. Took a black shawl from a pocket, and put that on. Huge round dark glasses, too. Turned, and with her back to the sales counter, smiled to the white wall before her, reached behind her, took the boxed glass poodle from off the counter and put it with receipt in her coat pocket, turned, took three steps toward the back of the store and stopped. The manager stood up behind the counter — he'd missed the show — and seeing her, asked, using the form of the title followed by her surname, would that be all? She replied — her back was to him —

"Isn't it enough?"

The manager came out from behind the counter and glanced at Red and at the salesman. Both men were cool, and each had a thin smile. The woman waved her index finger at the manager — her face was in profile, and as though claws had taken hold beneath her eyes and — yanked, she beckoned the manager to her, and with fingertip to her lips she led him a few steps away, stopped, moved so close he had to bend backwards, his eyes were something to see, she pressed closer, he bent back farther, she raised her left foot behind her, went up on tiptoe on her right foot, and putting her lips to his ear and her left hand on his chest, while she clenched and unclenched her right fist, whispered to him —

His face turned crimson with a smile, and he turned, took a few steps to his right, removed a pink Pussy Galore (lettered in black, with blue outline) sweatshirt from a box, walked over to the salesman at the counter and said giftwrap it, returned to the woman, and they assumed their former closeness as she whispered and he bent back, the salesman folded the sweatshirt in lime and then orange tissue, put it in a scarlet box, folded the tissue over and put on a yellow lid she stopped whispering, still so close to the manager's body he was almost doubled backwards, eyes glazed in rage, her lips parted showing perfect white false teeth, she said, his teeth were perfect, and real, and bared — "Amazing, isn't it?"

"It's fantastic," he said.

They laughed, tilting their chins up red lips peeling over sparkling ivories in a ripple of silent applause, she took his arm and they moved to the cash register, she spotting the salesman who was selecting a ribbon to go round the box, — cried, aghast — "Oh no, darling — not *yet!*"

And as the manager's normal color returned to his face, the blood ran out of the salesman's. She took from her purse, which was on the counter, her wallet from which she removed a business card, and as the manager cleared a space and the salesman fought fury, she took off her dark glasses and grey gloves, put them on the counter, and reaching again into her bag took out reading glasses from a sequined lavender cloth case, and laying the case on the counter, put on her reading glasses, reached for the ballpoint pen (Bic) that the salesman handed her. The manager, the salesman, and Red exchanged glances, and on being asked Red said he had merchandise for the buyer. Well. Did he have an appointment?

"Yes."

49

The manager flipped a switch and spoke into a concealed intercom, listened a moment, switched off and said the buyer was with another salesman. Would Red wait?

You bet.

He took off his jacket and scarf and – hat, glanced down at the bag of his goods, and stood there. Three men and one woman did not move, like green eyes and glass boots in London.

Two mothers with two daughters came into the store, and not looking to the right or to the left, marched back to the restaurant, each ordering the $5.00 hotdog special with rootbeer.

The door opened and a tall, very thin gentleman in the shape and color of a cadaver, entered the store, and joined the ladies at their table not missing the chance to glance at the manager and at the salesman, both of whom exchanged glances as the man passed, his yellow eyes floating in his face as he swept down the bright white tunnel followed by two direct stares.

Red smiled.

But then the door opened, and a girl came in followed by a woman with hard eyes and a black gloved hand on the girl's shoulder as the girl, in no visible way, maybe seventeen? knew the score, her wide, dark and haunted eyes did, and though so young her lined face and downdrawn lips showed the strain of that understanding: hands straight down at her sides almost glistened, and the spread of rigid fingers showed the evidence – preceding her who possessed her, for perhaps a banana split? to mix with the liquid in the corners of her possessor's mouth while, it was noticed, the woman in reading glasses smiled, her hands flashed in the air and she dashed off a note on her business card, handed it to the salesman who put the card in a small cream-colored envelope, put the envelope in the center of the box on top of the Pussy Galore sweatshirt, and while she put her glasses away, and put her dark glasses and gloves on, he re-folded the tissue paper, put the lid back on and tied a gold ribbon round the box, fashioned an elaborate bow, and with open scissors zipped the blade along the ends of the ribbon to achieve a cheerful array of curls. He handed the box to her with a professional smile and his eyes in slits. She was leaving.

The manager walked her to the door, and as he reached to open it, she cried –

"The blue!"

His eyes narrowed, his lips pursed, and as his shoulders jerked, he moved to a glass case just inside the door, opened it and took out a small blue mirror set in an ornate oval goldplated frame as she lowered

50

her dark glasses.

"That isn't blue," she said.

"It," the manager, with a soft growl: "is *emerald.*"

"It looked blue through my glasses!"

"Quite so." Razor edged. "We have them in blue, if you —"

As he reached to open a small box, the woman fixed her dark glasses in place, and with package under arm crushing the bow, she opened the door and left the store the manager paralyzed, holding the little box in his hand, so frozen one touch would shatter, and in that sense, the three men formed a tableau.

Thus the woman in dark glasses, with "a little cough" was gone into the day — or the evening, rather, for the day was over. The manager returned the box to its glass case, walked back to the cash register, and stood, staring down at the counter, face skull white.

"She forgot her receipt for the sweatshirt!" cried the salesman.

The manager rolled his eyes to the ceiling, then closed them, lowered his head, took a deep breath, gripped the counter, choked —

"Mail it to her."

51

Goodnight Irene

I WAS WAITING to get a haircut, and saw him outside, on the sidewalk. He glanced in and saw me.

What did you do?

I went outside and said hello!

Well.

How is he? I asked.

Hasn't changed at all: plump at forty, Tony Curtis in slacks and sportsjacket still doing the talking.

Is he bartending?

No.

"I quit there a year ago," he said. Eyes sleepy.

"The joint on upper Lex," I said. "What happened?"

"Do you want to hear?"

"You know."

"I was fired," he grinned. We walked around the corner into a bar and ordered, and as we drank I watched Tony trying to find a beginning.

"I made some money, but it was a terrible place."

"They're pretty bad."

"Coffins," he observed. "Smoke?" "No, thanks." Tony lit up a slender green low tar filter saying the clientele was a mix of bums on welfare or unemployment and the usual Lex tough guys and their girls. The owner a bastard you wouldn't believe. His lips thinned.

"No buybacks," I said.

"Yeah, but even so I made my money."

I wondered if that was why he was fired. He chuckled, sipped his drink and blew smoke over my shoulder.

"You gotta hear this," he said.

Okay.

"I'd been there a couple of years," he began. "It's a miracle I lasted that long. I got to know just about everybody in the neighborhood, so I could spot a stranger, and one night a guy comes in, sits down

53

and orders vodka twister rocks water chaser, no ice in the chaser. Got it?"

I said yes and he said,

"You and me, we've been around, right? Well, nobody will ever figure it out, but after one look at that creep, I hated his guts."

He looked at me.

"You know me," he said. "I'm a nice guy, right? Sure I am, I mean it, am I wrong? Tell me!"

I punched him in the shoulder and said he was a nice guy. "What happened."

"You always were a good listener."

"You always told good stories."

He liked that. He nodded. Got a distant look. Thought out loud: "But that guy was ter-a-bull to see I mean he was *terrible*."

Lips in a curl.

"His hands were long, so were his fingers, and his fingernails too, long, broken, and dirty, bad teeth, filthy all over. Never shaved. Sixty, over sixty, too old to look like that Goddammit that's right because I said it's right and I'm not kidding, that guy was a fuckin' *bum*," he paused, and under his breath: "a side order bananas."

"Maybe that was part of that."

"Bananas about cats?"

"Cats!"

"Cats! I know — cats, but that guy, I don't know how many he had, but he always came in with two, one on each shoulder, and while he drank they walked around on his shoulders, slept, or played in his crummy sweater, stuck onto him even when he went to piss. I think he had about a dozen because he rotated, Lucy and Fannie on Saturday night, and well I can't — won't remember their names, fuck 'em, I'm glad to forget! His name was Stan."

I smiled.

"It wasn't funny," he grinned. "The guy began to get to me, and you know me, I've been around, right? Right, so it took some doing, like — I mean it took forever for him to pay me. You know how I work — you know?"

He could make a martini with his left hand, a tom collins with his right while serving a beer and beginning a bloody mary, he got so hyped he couldn't stop to talk, and it infuriated him when customers didn't pay in his rhythm. "I know," I said.

"Okay," he said, putting his cigarette out, and ordering two more saying, "let me get these. I won at the track yesterday," watching the aged bartender make two languid drinks. "I'm even," Tony said, "and that guy sure is slow."

But Tony was in thought.

"He didn't come in often, twice a week at most, but always with his two cats, around ten, ten-thirty at night Jesus he was terrible. Tall, talltall, skinny with a caved-in face, long ratty hair, yellow kind of eyes with the whites — photo — brown — "

"Sepia."

"Yeah, sepia, and he always sat in the same spot — at the bar — on his barstool, to get smashed out of his skull, and leave around three with a quarter on the bar for my tip."

"Two bits," I murmured.

"Two fuckin' bits," he said, face reddening. "And on top of that, around midnight he starts coming on for buybacks, and you get it. I say look, I can't do that, I'll get fired, right?"

"Right."

"This is store policy, don't you get it? But he *didn't* get it, he kept on well no, *over* a year and I was beginning to flip — me! even when I *saw* him yeah but but then I began to wonder how I was gonna unload the dirty laundry, right? right, and one night, one night I noticed that the last thing he did was to drink the whole water chaser before he left. I noticed it."

"It seemed to mean more than it did."

"Real clear, but everything he did did because he was one of those lush bums who budget themselves down to their last nickel, aw you know. I know you know."

"I know," I said.

"I knew it," he said, "and not long after I'd noticed that last thing he did, one night he came in as usual, cats on his back and his skin like rotten meat, and on the second drink he starts begging me for a freebie, hey come on, please, I'm a poor man, can't you give me just one drink? and I thought I was gonna freak, the owner at the other end of the bar watching *me* say no, if you're broke, go home. I'm not broke, the guy said, I'm poor, buy me a drink, please. Please. Listen, I say, I'm not gonna lose this job over a fuckin' bum like you, or anybody else either, you want a drink, you pay for it, got it? do you want a drink? I want a drink, he says. Free. No way, I said. Case closed. All right, he said, I'll pay, and I poured it and moved down the bar to other customers while he dug dough out of his pocket, in nickels and dimes — pennies, too! while he stirred the vodka around until some of the ice melted and it looked like a double is how it went until

55

around three maybe earlier smasherrooney, cats on his shoulders, he went to the pisser, came back, sat down, and while they got settled again, he put two bits on the bar, finished his drink, smiled singing Goodnight Irene, and knocked back the whole glass of water, held onto the bar and the barstool, stood up, and staggered out the door."

"Nothing new."

"Nothing new except that I knew something had to happen but didn't know what." He finished his drink.

I did too.

"Let me get these," I said.

"I can smell him," he whispered. "I was so sick of that son of a bitch I didn't know what to do. I couldn't just—"

"No."

"You could see the dirt on him, and he smelled of catpiss, you could almost taste him, and when he pleaded with me, begged me—I'll tell you, the nice guy I am, went away, disappeared. Poof! and somebody else came in."

"Why didn't you refuse him? Bars have that right."

"That's true," he agreed. "But that guy did spend his dough, and though he was the worst creep in the place he had plenty of company! The women liked his cats and aw shit I mean that guy and that place give me the *shivers!* Stay out of the Lex bars!"

"I will indeed," I said, paying the bartender, we clinked glasses, and sipped. "Thanks," he said. "What happened?" I asked.

His eyes were hard with a glint: he said, "One night a guy came in, a regular, but who only drank the Russian—Stolichnaya hundred proof—sat next to Cat Man I gave the guy his usual, and they start talking about cats Jesus cats cats cats, the place got crowded, everybody knew each other and because I was so busy I kept the Russian in the speedrack, okay?"

"Okay."

"Okay, the night went on, pimples and whiskers that fuckin' bum talking about his cats, to his cats, customers petting them and something told me tonight was the night. I didn't know what I was going to do, or how—or what would happen, but something was in the air. I went on, as usual, until around midnight I began giving him doubles, working very fast, shifting around so the owner couldn't see me, and around one old Catboy was pretty loaded—ahead of schedule—and by two so wasted he couldn't much talk, or much walk, so when he stood up to take a leak he pointed to his drink and sang Goodnight Irene, thanks for being so kind, his eyes almost crossed, seeing those doubles double, maybe, and staggered back to the men's room. But because the guy who drank the Russian had just gone home — smashed — the bottle was still in the speedrack, and I took the pourer out of the bottle, and while filling Catcreep's rock glass to the brim with eighty bar vodka, an easy triple, I emptied the chaser glass of water and filled it with the Russian hundred, put the pourer back in, returned the bottle to its normal place on the shelf behind me, and served other customers until Katzo came back, fished round in his pockets for my two bits, found it, put it on the bar, and stood, weaving around, picked up the rock glass and drank it. His eyes popped open, what a surprise! but he shuddered, breathed deep, found balance, thanked me, said goodnight, raised and drained the water glass."

I a little gagged.

"Unh huh," he said, "that's right. At first he stood there. Then he retched, and a little dribbled out of his mouth, but he wanted to keep it, the hardboiled lushes don't want to lose any of it, and while his stomach heaved, he fought for control, the blood ran out of his face, pale as a corpse. He turned to his right in staggering, jerky motions, and by holding onto backs and shoulders of other customers — they were used to him! — he made his way to the door while the cats adjusted to his lurching, but just in front of the door he stopped, put both hands on his chest and jacknifed, slammed his face on a tabletop and fell sideways onto the floor as the cats jumped free. Somebody helped him up, put the cats back on him, and walked to the door with him, as he bent forward, hugging himself, a guy opened the door, he pitched forward, bounced off the doorjamb, and stumbled outside."

My voice was soft. "Did he die?"

"Who knows? Fuck him. I was fired that night."

"So you never saw him again."

"I never saw him again, that catfucker. Listen, I gotta go. I gotta date and I gotta go home and clean up. Lend me your pen and I'll give you my new address and phone number. Let's get together again, and you do the talking. Okay?"

"Sure," I said, handing him my pen.

Good

IN ONE VOICE the woman told her she didn't know what her voice sounded like, suggesting the use of a tape recorder, admitting it was a shame
to have to turn to machines.

Well, that didn't come only as a surprise, it also came as a puzzle,
for she or, as she continued to anticipate her therapist telling her to
stop (as usual), doing this or that, little things form patterns, on the
bus uptown she thought about this newest news, and figured out it —
the tape machine — was a bridge to *him:* the problems she was having
with that guy were, she pondered, verging on obsession, and the doctor was tired of hearing her talk about how he felt — how did *she* feel?
Her heart warmed in sympathy for the doctor. They have to listen to
talk talk and more talk, day and night, oh the message was clear, it
was a wonder they didn't fall asleep (this is what it meant when they
yawned: they're always alert), in an inner growl saying she had a problem with that guy, that non-communicative, narrow-minded, mute
creep who not only didn't talk to her, but didn't pay any attention to
her, which came up in therapy again and again, but she never got tired
of talking about it, because — this too was discussed — she was, in a little
way, fascinated by him and, she admired him. He might be silent, but
he supported her at every turn, and he let her alone. He enjoyed going
out, he liked subtle surprises, and his dry but funny sense of humor
amused her no end which, this too emerged, was as if she laughed at
herself, yet somehow it wasn't enough — she might, she admitted, be
one-sided about it, but she felt she wasn't getting more, as *most* didn't
satisfy, she was, the doctor chided, the kind who wanted it all.

Which made her guilty, yet on the same plane she admired the doctor for that cool wit, while hating her for making her guilty. Resented
her! That's what it was.

"I resent that," she said.

"You do?"

The question trick! They never get enough, she thought. Never.
Cried —

"You're too objective!"

"I am?"

"Oh stop it!" she cried. "That's unfair!"

The woman seemed puzzled.

Another trick.

"I have a love/hate relationship with my therapist," she told him, ignoring the syllables.

He nodded.

"Can I tell you about it?" she asked, "or will you go into your usual three-monkey act."

He made a thin smile, to the familiar reference, the way she said it as if she'd tell him anyway or, wished she could, that's what she wanted, which made her defensive, anxious and, in that order, angry. She knew who and what she was angry at, too, and she knew he knew (he did), which irritated the hell out of her, because it wasn't him, it was her. It was as if he kept waiting, but he couldn't say it, no. Wouldn't. He waited for her. It seemed up to her. It was up to her. She had to say it all. Everything.

Her follow up thought ran like this.

I've got to do something about it.

Watching the evening news and having a beer, waiting for her to come home from her shrink's, he too was thinking.

He knew he had a problem, not easy to articulate everyman's thought structure, and because he had learned, in the usual vicarious manner, good cause for fiction, — from her experience in therapy, a word he hated, he had gathered the possibility that he didn't like himself, and though it wasn't clear to him, except to make him uncomfortable and anxious, around the corner ahead of him was the further possibility somewhere, the source of his silence, not so much as a whisper, though it was in a way, but as a hint, and because he wasn't an introspective person, not much followed after. He was and he liked it, a man of few words, not taking into consideration his fear.

He smiled.

He frowned.

"But," she would ask: "can't you even say that, *that* you're a man of few words?"

No, therefore confusion, and gloom, which he thought unfair. He didn't pretend to live on inner terms, he was too positive or — what was it? His process was involved with what would happen next, he took what was going on as a matter of course, and without expectation, in a hopeful attitude, though silent, he was secure in what would come, and her willing, eager, introspective halting, shifting, changing, leaping advances and setbacks on psychiatric searchings shook what he had made sure of since childhood, and thus he feared her, the second of his two fears, and in all of the whole storm, that he didn't like himself caused him to admire her, even envy her, because he loved her energy and above all her passion.

Happy and drunk in a cab coming home from a party, he looking forward to getting home, and she for some reason depressed, gave him a long look, and asked him if he knew how to sing.
He looked at her.
He smiled.
His lips parted.
"I've got a crush on you," he sang, adding, —
"Sweetie Pie."
Her heart skipped a beat, her brain got fuzzy, she whispered as they embraced and kissed, aw
"I'm nuts about you."

"But *why* must I understand?"
"I didn't say understand," the doctor said, "I said compromise."
The patient's epidermal structure turned red.
"I'm sorry," she murmured.
The doctor sighed, ah, not an altogether open sigh, but not altogether hidden, either, for she wanted to give her patient a little obvious clue. They'd been through this.
But the patient was forlorn.
"I don't know what to do," she said.
"You don't know what to do?" the woman asked. "You don't know what compromise is?"
"But I made a slip. I said understand."
The doctor lit a cigarette, sat back and stared at her patient, then spoke:
"Is that bad? An unconscious translation of compromise to understand? I've heard worse!"
The patient downward gazed, lower lip appearing, saying,
"You want me to compromise with him?"
"I want you to realize you can't have everything, and compromise is a means to that realization."
"He won't compromise."

61

"How do you know? Your silence might provoke his speech." The doctor leaned forward. "Do you know what your voice sounds like?"

Soft response: "No."

"Do you want me to tell you?"

"Do you want to?"

The doctor laughed.

"No, but I can. Do you want me to?"

Well! Here it is! Case history two hundred and thirty five, which she realized was his street address, *thousand*, she growled.

"No," she answered.

"Good," the doctor said, looking angry, causing the patient to wonder what good meant.

She looked at the doctor.

The doctor looked back.

"All right," said the doctor, "get hold of a tape machine."

She did. At Macy's.

And when she thought she was practicing compromise and a little reciprocity with him, she turned on the machine.

But he didn't know it.

Watching boxing on tv. He liked boxing. She hated boxing. They watched in silence. After the tenth round he told her he had been a fighter in high school.

She was so irritated she didn't know what to do. She forgot about the tape machine. Exasperated. Loathed boxing. She exploded, remembered the tape, forced control, got reasonable, went into the kitchen for two more beers, turned off the tape, returned and apologized.

That night while he slept, she listened to herself. Or, she crept into the kitchen, ran the tape back to the beginning, and in a fantasy of telephoning her doctor to say she was frightened, she heard her doctor say that word.

Silence. And following a little static and some mumbling, voices cleared and, she couldn't believe what she was hearing, her blood seemed to reverse and her body crimsoned, and crystallized into sound and she cringed from the whining, complaining, arrogant, hostile, *hateful* —

Click.

"I'll never say another word," she said.

It began:
Shu Yu

He thought:
Let me see
as he typed.

Worked on a new novel, dashed off a short story, and was running out of smokes when she came home he forgot to write, he typed, that he'd phoned her at work and asked her to bring home a pack which she did, and after she did, or, as a consideration in the pouring rain "I'll go for beer."
She said.
He said don't be silly. "I'll go."
He did.
They drank beer, went to a Szechuan restaurant for supper, each had two drinks and after delicious seafood and vegetable soup, enjoyed cold beer hot ginger lamb sneezes scallions, shrimp with black bean sauce followed by kumquats (for her) and pistachio ice cream (with cherries) for him with a shot of straight bar vodka on the side for both of them, alongside of which the waiter a cool kid a natural salesman backed her up with vodka rocks, as a gift:

Be sincere

her fortune read: even when you don't mean it.
She thanked him, meaning it. (#211)

But the man eating the pistachio ice cream wondered why the waiter hadn't given him a drink on the house, yet following his fortune (#41), he let it pass, for as it turned out, when they received the bill they checked the total and the waiter hadn't charged him:

What the eye does not see
The heart does not grieve for.

Home with a half pint, two nips each and off to a movie the title of which was as he typed unnecessary, the cuts and camera angles were fantastic, Meeker was fine, the rain stopped and they dropped into the RENO for a couple. Talked and drank with the pleasant bull bartender built like a slick softball crewcut soft as puppy's hair: a plus for that New Jersey mugstate, Del, by name: came home, had nips and smoke with downstairs neighbor Bob, and after in part staggering and floating up the stairs, a fast nip and to bed comma dash best sleep he'd had in days awakened late by the harsh street door buzzer, pushed the button, neighbor Bob! with five cases of beer — he'd got a bargain: *and* green on white: a cartoon seal. The small waxed paper unfolded: an eyeopener through a plastic straw, *very* smooth. Up a wide wide Avenue to photos of Victorian Asia at Japan House, west to Macy's for all kinds of things: chill Saturday. Snow white.

Snappy day.

One hundred dollars a gram.

"Let's get some," she said.

Blue skies.

They did.

Great.

Into the store, and she was cool. Shopping for Christmas? Maybe.

Well, it was the season. Or, it was her season. Any season was. She was any season anywhere and she was looking good. Calm. Composed. What she was thinking was beyond the salesman, but she was thinking, and! it was twelve days before Christmas! as she inspected the glassware section, she might be buying presents maybe for *him*, for mom and dad, or maybe for herself, or — anyway, she didn't buy anything. Nothing seemed to strike her fancy. Just shopping around.

Her hat was peaked and of thick tan and white fur, and seen from behind, a plait of thick brown hair laid down her spine, tips bound by a red rubber band. Her skin was white with a rose tint suggesting the north countries.

She wore a British Army Officer's leather belt that went around her waist and chest connected by diagonal straps. Brass buckles. Her sweater was very heavy, the color of Atlantic salt and chunks of black pepper, tucked in at the waist above very heavy chocolate corduroy pants that were tucked into high-laced, square-toed, oxblood leather boots polished to a mirror shine. She didn't seem to breathe while she walked, she rather glided across the floor, she had a wild body under all those clothes, ah yes indeed, and for added spice, imbedded in the right nostril of her semitic nose, a gold bead twinkled, perhaps in friction with her downward gaze.

On a glass shelf before her, a box lay wrapped in thin clear plastic. The box displayed four glass mugs that were eye-catchers, to catch her eye they had to be special, and they were, because they weren't just glass mugs, they were small glasses tucked into small brass, copper-rimmed mugs with handles, she liked things that tucked, we know what tucking is, tuck tuck! she raised the plastic off the box, and with long and elegant fingers, the nails of which were opaque pink and trimmed, no polish, she picked a mug from its place, and using both hands separated the glass from its copper container, looked deep into the one, and then into the other, fitted them together, raised it to her lips and sipped, thought a moment, then replaced the mug, folded the plastic over the box, tucked in the corners, and without a glance at the salesman, who stood not two feet away, watching, fascinated, she floated outside.

Downstairs, in the shipping room in the basement of the store, Junior was telling Joss about a dance the night before, and while Harvey was upstairs telling the salesman to go down into the stockroom, and bring up a cherry Baats vase, the announcer for a radio rock station said that not since 1879, an even hundred years ago, had the temperature been so high — 68, and, he added, there was a chance that the record would be broken. Was it? Who knows! But, in a real little mystery, somewhere in the pre-Christmas city of hordes wandered a woman looking like Sweden, Daniel Boone, Ghandi, Hitler, Mountbatten, and Hollywood all tucked in to climb the Alps on a record breaking hot day, guys and girls walking around in jeans and t-shirts, she stopped in a store for a sip of invisibility, then floated away, outside again, as the salesman unwrapped the box, took out the same glass and copper mug, and sipped, raised his eyes in thought, returned the mug to the box, folded the plastic back in place, tucked in the corners, and with his eyes on the front door, he licked his lips.

Bill Thistle bought Mr & Mrs Frank Thistle (his folks), one glass icicle to go to 59 Stonehedge, Tarpon Springs, Florida. $2.50 plus $1.75 shipping.

For Dr & Mrs Lewis Scribner, he bought one Bayberry candle to go to R D Burburry Lane, Manlius, NY. $2.00 plus $1.75 shipping.

He also bought Mrs Frances Thistle (his wife) one glass icicle, to go to Rochester, Michigan. $2.50 plus $1.75 shipping.

Banka stop 'em: oh-kah, odka, ah-ba kettle rattle sink 'em *bam!* Fluck 'em (forget 'em). Vostum! Podka! That's my vodka! 90 yards to go. Shipping, noodles, oodles *bingo* lingo, two bits, four bits, critics peek! What they don't know (up this creek) is over and over a quarterback sneak!

Michelina Keeler Snibbe bught a box of cookies for Mabel
Bennett in Coral Gables, Florida. $7.05 plus $2.00 shipping.

She also bought, for Paul Snibbe, in Los Angles, California,
one salad bowl set: $21.50 plus $3.25 shipping.

And for James Snibbe, in North Scituate, Mass., the same,
plus $2.00 shipping.

For Robert Snibbe in Clearwater, Florida, one (1) box of
cookis ($7.05 plus $2.00 shipping).

And another box of cookies to be sent to George Snibbe, in
Laguna Hills, CA. Same, plus $3.00 shipping.

Epyme O. Cawthorne will pick up twenty fruit cakes.

The Brothers Warm

ON THE HILL beyond the cornfield, cows were meandering down toward the corn where they were *not* supposed to go. I sat up, yawned and stretched, and feeling my sore tongue, was reminded I'd lost a filling the night before, and as there was a picnic at Roger and Bobbie's farm that afternoon, I remembered Terry had made an appointment with the dentist, in town, for me before the picnic.

We got there early. Terry left me on the sidewalk in front of the front door, then drove away to pick up two students, Allison and Marion, who were waiting by the drugstore. Terry would take them out to the picnic, and in an hour or so return for me.

On a one hundred degree day in Mansfield, Pennsylvania.

Deserted in the heat, almost.

Upstairs, to the left and I was in the waiting room waiting for Dr. Coole, had a nice talk with a teenage farm boy, lit a smoke, glanced out the window at quiet country loners on small town sidewalks, and noticed that the sign across the street, placed in clear view between two large pine bushes: *The Kuhl Funeral Home*, and as the boy from the farm talked about his two brothers, one on Guam and the other just out of the Navy and disgusted with himself, which amused his (the) younger brother, I thought I'd mention the cool coincidence to the dentist and, when, at last, I was admitted to the *inner sanctum* I told him I wanted a temporary filling, he said there wouldn't be any problem, and after picking around the hole, and cleaning it, causing me considerable perspiration, he made a mix that'd fill it up. I mentioned the sign across the street and he laughed, saying if we don't get you they sure will, and we chuckled. Dr. Coole had a nice smile, and a nice laugh, too. He was in his late thirties, I thought, and around six feet tall. Thin, shy. His voice was middle state, and he spoke soft, tended to drop the g from ing which reminded me of a woman I know from Australia, and as he bent over and put the soft filling in, I saw how clear and direct his eyes were, and felt how warm his presence was, as he sang, just above a hum, a sort of musical whisper, a song I hadn't heard like

71

that for almost twenty years, from a man in dark glasses on a stage in a dark blue nightclub who had stood under overhead cones of red light, and on his trumpet played the lyric, and Dr. Coole, just off the one word, sang it soft, and clear, just like Miles:

singin' songs of love
but not for me

End Dust

GREEN.

Green.

Avocado green, green all over, bald as a cucumber, and seven feet tall. Her skull almond-shaped, and her wide set of eyes blue, her cheeks round. Her fingernails and toenails black and shiny, earlobes pink, luminous, her inner thighs and armpits apple green, as the nape of her neck, palms of her hands and bottoms of her feet. She was a shy person, and if embarrassed exuded an odor not unlike petunias, for she had nectar in her veins, yet though shy, she was enthusiastic, and if in a public place she sneezed, onlookers might notice, for the nostrils of her small nose were yellow rimmed and her snot popsicle orange. She winked one blue eye at him as he handed her a lemon hanky. Thin, blood red lips stretched from ear to ear causing a slight crevice in the center, a glimpse of .teeth as white as snow, and just then, the tip of her tongue — just the tip, seen, too, of the color of oysters, and much the same texture.

Nku, and blew her nose, folded the hanky, tucked it in the pocket of her lavender dress, and stepped up onto the avenue —

Mya kweepit?

Zoo, yah exel-bissionisd, he teased, taking her hand, they walked up the avenue, on the avenue, looking in store windows, once stopping to purchase slices of watermelon, which they ate on the way to the wild, and after strolling through shattered glass and twisted steel, went to a film: geography of spheres the seven colors of Tad in the breath of the earth. He was a few inches taller than she, his skin the color of shale, and seemed, in a certain light, to have scales. His head was low on his shoulders, and like the profile of an egg, quite large, but his shoulders were small, and his torso and legs very long, he seemed a bulb on a stalk, except that his eyes were three: two green discs flanked a midnight blue inset, oval, above his blunt, yellow ochre snout. His

73

mouth was small, and lips terra cotta around double rows of tiny teeth of the color and sparkle of rubies. His hands and feet were large and splayed, without nails. His private parts were the tint of inner conch, and like his long, pink enamel tongue, tended to unfurl.

Why, he wondered, did she want to have hair?

He Did

A POSTCARD from Zack

Dear jos
I porably wont be home for Xms, so tell Nan that please as I gota lot of work todo here as in other places   so I wont be able to be home whic you undorstand am sure.

A postcard to Zack

Dear Zack,
Well you better get home on Christmas 'cause Mom's been sick, and we need you as we know the kind of work you do you can take a couple of days and get here.

A postcard from Zack

Dear Jos
I know what Mom's sick of the same as you do shes sick of that same old thing and im busy as I canbe. Ill let you know.

A postcard to Zack

Zack there are words id say to you face I cant put on this card Doc was by this am and Mom's in the hospital I'm maddern hell at you you come home.

A postcard from Zack

Dear Jos yes I can imagine what youd say to me but i have to say to you that my jobisk ping me here and il cant get of, ill be home for newyears

77

& in return:

OK Zack you take one step onto the steps of this hose ill blow yuor brains out Mom died last night cant you telephone?

Therefore:

Dear Jos ill be home Xms am very sorry.

And:

You come home Zak your dead.

* * *

"What are you gonna do?"
"I don't know," Zack said, and the bartender poured him another shot, adding a head on his beer.
"Why didn't you go home in the first place?"
"I couldn't," Zack said.
"Why?"
"Well you know that son of a bitch Bill Donner he had us on forty-eight hour shifts, and my turn came on Christmas."
"You could have told him your Mom was dying—"
Zack rubbed his crewcut, and said "I used that one before, when I went to see you know who in Memphis."
The bartender nodded, a comprehending hm expression on his face, but he asked, What'd your Mom die of, —
Tell him, I told Zack.
"It was drinkin', that old woman drank herself to her grave every day, my brother Jos is a chickenshit son of a bitch and my sister hates my guts, always has. My Mom was in the hospital so often they built it around her and the doctors didn't know how she stayed livin' she was so crazy. If I'd of gone home whenever she was sick I might as well have lived there which was one of the reasons I got out, and why should I have gone back where they hate me?"

The bartender looked at Zack, and wondered if it was Zack talking, or the stuff that had killed Zack's Mom.

"Well," the bartender advised — an amiable country fella — "If I was you, I'd stay away from home."

"If I was me," Zack frowned, "I would too."

"I'm kind of a one-person person."

—Doris Day

Pomp and Circumstance

ONE LATE SPRING while Korea was warming up, a boy almost a man made a decision that cost him his life, therefore, as the gates of Watergate broke loose, and the boy was indeed a man, he told a minister, who stood at his bedside in the hospital, that he was sorry, went into coma, and that was that.

The minister, a sharp fellow, with a pragmatic turn of mind, knew what the dead man had meant, yet realized there was more here than a confessed regret. There always is. But . . .

"I wonder," he murmured.

***

After having graduated from high school, the man who died had fallen in love with a girl who had meanwhile fallen in love with him, thus they were married, and within but two repeats of the four seasons, two children appeared in their lives.

A boy, and a girl.

The dead man was not tall, but lean, with dark curly hair, a ready smile—handsome in the extreme, and having been influenced by his mother's wit, as well as her sense of humor, he was in brief the toast of the town.

Even in a literal sense, adding to the imaginative, standing in line with him at the bank—everyone loved him. He had, as was said, his mother's charm, his father's bold handsomeness and sensitivity, as well as his own given beauty.

His wife was a dark-haired looker with a figure and aura to drive men to dreams. A common sense woman, and (and this is sad), loved her husband beyond dreams, yet likewise, feared him in that way.

His devastating mother-charm.

He had a good job, popular as ever—there seemed no end to it— had taken social drinking home with him, at first it was fun, at second, on the good job he had, it was a charmed life, at third it was a habit and at home he lost her. Vietnam was warming up.

In and out of hospitals, light sessions with psychologists, AA, his certain but desperate charm held him together from job to job, failure after failure, and in Nixon's second term, was taken to the hospital for what he knew was the final bid, his liver was gone, and feeling nothing — drugged to the end — at last breath gathered himself to confess to the minister that he was sorry, on the threshold of his tomb which, without another word, he entered.

"Did you know him well?" the minister asked.

"In high school," I said. "I knew his parents. We went to church together. He was an only child."

Mother brilliant, charming, outrageous in her humor, yet observant, and tender. A full-breasted woman with slender ankles and a loud laugh. His father was a plump, solid, shy and sensitive, very successful businessman, who smiled and sipped his drink, while his wife kept her audience in riot. But his eyes sparkled, watching her.

Vivid in my memory.

So it is a sad story.

The man who died had been all the things we imagine we want to be. In a complete identity he'd been wonderful, even his nervousness was charming, although in secret he was a shy and frightened person, tense, edgy, running around end, and who, perhaps too soon, sought out and made the legal commitment with her who adored him, and soon feared his fear.

There are two stories in which he figures. Ask, next we meet.

It seemed amazing. His mom, dad — charming and successful parents with their bright and handsome son, who, with his beautiful wife, drank as a group together, at first fun, but with two children, drinking became another person, a member of the family hard to keep up with, and, in a strange way for those of us who knew him — after college, and having been an officer in Korea — seeing him at The Ten Mile House, something was missing, as replaced by something else, and with the exception of his wife and children who left him, and he went home to mom and dad and from hospital to hospital, AA and psychologists, he kept up with the other fella, the seeming-new, member of the family without the wife and kids, until something missing blew the whistle, and his body realized

The End.

"He was a marvelous but tragic boy, with all that he was, and all that he had, he hated himself, and perhaps his mother most of all, yet

84

his distant father too, not for the difficult love they gave him, but for the personality, which made him feel odd and of them, in them, a reproduction, so in panic he married, and no doubt feared his effect on his wife, as well as his children, for how could a reproduction reproduce something new? from a terror they'd be him, he who was already two? the mirror of his future reflecting the mirror of his past."

"So he began to drink?"

"For contact."

"Contact?"

"Touch to another. Alcohol, the organic link to his mind that knew what he felt." I paused. "Had felt all along."

The minister's eyes grew bright: "Do you believe," he asked, "that he wanted to marry his mother?"

"And divorce his father? No. He wanted to marry himself to lose both, and become what he'd missed."

Our eyes met.

"You mean he married so as not to murder?"

"Maybe. But it backfired. His mother took over his marriage, bragged about him when the children came, all the more for they were her grandchildren, and her son, in spite of it all, she chided, was a success, at which adults chuckled.

"Seen from afar the pattern seems simple, and to some it is, but after his wife and children left, and he was paying alimony and child-support, drinking more than ever, in and out of hospitals, his father had a heart attack, and died, and—"

"His mother died."

"No. The son died first—telling you he was sorry. Not days after, his mother died."

"That's right. I remember. Cancer."

"Yes," I said. "But she had lost her mind."

I looked out the window across the churchyard lawn, and the streets of Missouri-childhood beyond, thinking, remembering how we had loved him without envy—so rare—and, in those rosy high school days how darling and crazy he was about Sally Hopper, Pomp and Circumstance, and her the breathtaking blonde Queen of May.

I said:

"He was sorry for everything, for all he had been, and had not become,—his failure as a man, as a husband, and a father living in a day to day world like millions of others, and he had betrayed that, but at bottom the deepest grief of all—he had betrayed himself in the name of love, for it was himself whom he wanted to love, to love

85

himself in just that way we had loved him, but in part because he wouldn't dare, so too because he didn't know how, —"

The telephone rang.

A grim smile crossed my face.

The minister reached for the phone.

"Hello?"

Psychology

RIGHT OUT OF THE BLUE she called to say she was going to be in his neighborhood. Could they get together for a drink? They hadn't seen each other in a couple of years and that in passing.

Without hesitation he said yes, although he and his new girlfriend had made other plans, and she, the girlfriend, was furious. But that came a little later, because although he had said yes, without hesitation, he had asked the woman on the phone if, when they met, she would return a book — a first American edition — he had left with her a couple of years ago, and she agreed.

So he argued, to his sweetheart:

"I get a book I won't have to travel to the end of town to get, so I won't have to be with her, in her apartment again!"

There was no questioning that logic. His girlfriend admitted it was a golden shortcut, yet she was still angry because he had said yes without thinking of her and what they had planned for that day — Saturday, the first day of her weekend and Monday back to her Goddamned job and here he was meeting a woman he had loved ten years before, and hadn't seen for two.

"Look," he said, telling his girlfriend the name and location of the meeting place — "it's two blocks from where you're going to get the pattern and the material, so afterwards, meet me at the bar!"

To which she agreed, and, as it turned out, the day was great. They did everything they'd planned, and more, all very happy, yes, but her truth rang in his ears, and shook him in a way that made him both anxious and unsettled, because it was true, he had agreed to the meeting without hesitation, and, as his girlfriend pursued her deduction she mentioned that several months before, when his ex-wife had been in town and had called, he had agreed to see her without hesitation, too, meaning

"When they call, you jump," she finished.

True, no denying it, and he realized, in his turn, both women had a power over him to which, without hesitation, he deferred. He knew,

89

in secret, if he didn't, he'd be guilty and regretful, because, also in secret, he had thought of both women — not often, true — but he had, and as he was honest with himself, he knew why. Ah, Mom. If she beckoned — he obeyed, a problem compounded by the fact that although he jumped to her call in truth he was angry, not because he jumped — though that too! — but because to say no was to reject being manipulated — one of the reasons he said yes. Some habits can make a guy wonder if he is awake or not, and this, was one of those.

Oh the hours and money spent in therapy! so while he knew as much as he knew (he knew a lot) — the source, the pattern, his response-structure — what yet remained was, as his therapist had said, how to kick?

Then the doctor — after dropping that line about a circle of psychological women — had touched a nerve:

"What does she want?"

Good question! So good he couldn't answer it! but, he rationalized, he had his foot in the door, knowing, however, it was the kind of door that led to reflective illusions, and in all honesty, to other doors beyond, so to get through this one was only for openers. The big doors followed. A corny metaphor which he enjoyed.

* * *

He was punctual, as was she. They shook hands, kissed in brief, sat at a table, ordered drinks, began to talk and as usual, having known each other in every intimacy in verifiable continuity ten years before, yet not having seen each other in so long, they had a lot to say, therefore only a little got said. She gave him the book (200 De Maupassant stories), and seeing his obvious but cool pleasure she realized he had agreed to see her because he wanted the book, meaning, she knew, he had waited two years for a chance to get it, rather than call her and visit. That book! She felt hurt, and used. But in a way she despised, she told herself to be patient. Hadn't he used her before?

This was going on as they began talking. She knew he knew and he knew she knew, and what they also knew was once he got what he wanted he was happy, and, which caused her to feel trapped, when he was happy he was good to be with, therefore his will to be happy overwhelmed her, because when he was happy it was almost impossible not to be with him, for when he was happy he was everything she wanted in a man, thus her habit to bend to his will, while it pleased her in this case, it also, in fact, infuriated her which, she knew, was

90

a direct recall to her bending to her father's will — to be happy by the sacrifice of her own will was indeed — so it seemed — a problem of high order, yet it was as she knew, by heart as well as habit, as common as life itself, and in her rage and confusion, she used her habit as a weapon. She beckoned to men in classic, sincere, a warm *I'm yours* style. And if he, on his side, being anxious and without fail miserable, although he appeared to be happy, if he had any clear memories which he could call unpolluted, it was the memory of how they met that was most fresh, it had happened so fast he'd been breathless — although it wasn't long before they began to confuse each other, she him because he didn't know what she wanted, she didn't either, and while both knew what he wanted was to be with her in the way he wanted which was to be with himself as he pleased, with her at his side, doing not much else but drink, read books, go to a bar or two, watch tv, drink, listen to Mozart, talk, eat, talk some more, screw, sleep, screw, sleep, and wake up to begin it again, which led to the end of it. They couldn't spend two days in her apartment without fighting, he felt forced to leave, he angry, she furious, and both baffled. On and off, it went like that, and in a literal sense the calendar years leafed by, his wife divorced him, he left town, and in that process, while traveling had met his new sweetheart, but the woman sitting in her apartment half way up the east side, thinking her thoughts, was amazed if not stunned that the sweetheart he'd met was *still* his sweetheart! Two years with one woman? meaning, it was clear, he wouldn't be coming up to see her anymore. Interesting. Will she stay with him? How that guy could talk! And drink! Something to ponder — not that she pondered much, although she did, she thought of him once in a while but with every thought and memory came anger, and — baffled was she, because her anger pivoted on pleasure. It was *good* to be rid of him, although — he often wondered — was it true? Did she need him? No. Yes — she wanted him *to a point*, was she jealous of him? Yes. No — for it seemed the durability of an affair based on being jealous of the desired object will lead to its own dissolve, the subject (love) notwithstanding. A sore point, so sore in fact he dared not mention it, for she would scream to the highest heavens. But on the other hand, even if — all this — was true, did it affect her life? Not much, he thought. She was a busy, hardworking person, and in her life, friends, movies, the theatre, uptown parties — she was an uptown woman and he was a downtown guy (in that city they lived in, a real cause for consideration, and though neither of them ever thought of it, the real reason why it was no go from the start), which rationalization relieved him. Or did it?

***

What they said that afternoon isn't of this story, although a good slick writer could make a fine novella, or even a novel of it, given the apropos detail, background, and dialogue, all that stuff they say gives characters character, etc. This is of another story, *Psychology*, by Katherine Mansfield, which he happened to have read the night following the same afternoon he had met her in the bar, causing him to realize that the meeting, and the talk, was in reality a non-meeting centering on what was not said, and keeping it elusive, which was clear.

And did not confuse him. He thought it would, though, seeing her again, and talking. But it didn't, because it was clear that looking at each other, and talking, and thinking about it afterwards he realized she had realized he hadn't changed in the least, except for his haircut, which caused her considerable surprise, for it was short and messy with a youthful look she'd never seen.

While they talked he saw she too hadn't changed, although — he realized — she knew she had just as he knew he had, and in truth they both had changed, but not with each other. There was something that would never change (see above parenthesis), and when they parted each was relieved, each perhaps a little strange-feeling, because to part with a habit intact *is a strange experience*. That he had talked too much — which she hated — made him self-conscious and defensive which pleased her, and it did not please her, for she had used her old trick again, asking him the questions that would cause him to talk too much so she could hate him for all those words, yet to envy him for what he said, which was worth listening to, and when he in turn asked her his questions, and as always — with exceptions — she answered in brevity, it was in her style happening all over again, for she was at points demure.

That confused him.

So he knew, he knew as sure as Moll Flanders evolved into Becky Sharp becoming Scarlett O'Hara, in her relationship with him — no matter other men — her sudden softness, demure and beguiling femininity was, as long as he was near her, beyond change. She knew the magic it worked, she had seen the results, and the fact that, in all likelihood, it was a manipulated cover and antithetical to her true, firm, angry and passionate self being a challenge to him — she had a door of her own to open, a door as resisting as his, and he had said yes without hesitation. And she became demure. So they went their different ways, afterwards, each realizing each had confused the other through a

92

helpless but nonetheless effective means, more complicated — they imagined — than they dared believe.

Late that night he sat up in bed, reading. No doubt she was too. Yet he often put the book down, and thought, and thought, and wondered, feeling confused and angry, asking himself — What is it? Why is it all so complicated? Would he see her again? Under what circumstances? And what would they say? Would it be the same? Yes, of course, but what could he do to make it different? Goddammit, he thought, she's tough, so am I, but what can I do, is it up to me? Maybe that's it! It's up to me! and his heart sank, he stared across the room as his sweetheart slept beside him, her

> head on her pillow
> her hair all awry
> the curve of her cheek
> so new to him

— he felt an adolescent confusion and guilt, and from way back in his mind, a thought (he thought), came racing out with a clear field ahead, in objective logic, and perhaps cold, but clean clear through, fiercely:

Tell her, I said.

— He smiled! That's good! Good idea!

If I see her again, or if she phones or writes — no matter what. Tell her I can't see or make contact with her because she confuses me. She'll ask why but I'll say I don't know. When will you find out? she'll ask, and I'll answer (his lips thinned in the fantasy, his blood warming to the confrontation) — without hesitation:

I don't know. Maybe never, but no contact until —

He felt guilt because it would hurt her. So,

STAND FIRM! I cried

Darkly, firm? he agreed to that (he thought) thought, be resolute because she'll ask if, when my confusion is over, we can meet again?

I don't know, but the odds are against it.

You mean you don't want to see me — ever. Her voice will be flat.

If you think that clears my head, you're wrong, I'll say, and then so long. Take care of yourself. But.

That — *that* little thought was almost vicious, and he paled as he sat in bed, trying to rationalize it with the old I'll-at-last-have-said-it business, meaning I can be objective about her. My shoulder to my door, free to push my way into — into what?

93

To bigger doors in an unlit sky, like hers to her, toward a dull gleam in a steel cliff where I'll push, shove and kick, using the crowbar and sledgehammer of my will, and be face to face with no one but me, just as she faces her door in her way. But not mine, he determined—then thinking he lied! Had he? Yes.

Well.

Him

THE CORPORATE EXECUTIVE sat at his desk, staring at the opposite wall. Seeing very little this morning, and thinking even less, as a storm of emotion swept through him.

The face!

That laugh!

"Hi!" that old childhood friend had cried: "Can it be true? Is this face you? That's a poem," and the man had laughed, beaming as they shook hands.

No, he said to his wife, who had never met the man, yet in three decades of marriage, had heard the name. No, the corporate executive had said, a chilled whiskey sour in his hand, and himself in his armchair, facing his wife, who sat on the sofa across from him — "He hasn't changed at all."

That felt good.

"He still acts a boy. Remember? I showed you his Christmas card." Pause. "A woodcut."

"We'd been to Chicago," she said. Finding pleasure.

"Yes."

He paused.

"Chicago."

"Are you all right?"

"Of course," he lied. "I'm a little tired."

She didn't believe him. She liked that, too.

"It was a long day."

They knew.

It wasn't the mystery of her sex that knew both were liars, or that they themselves knew it, or that it was part of an executive's life. Common sense said so. But his face and eyes were different, and the eyes in her sex saw it.

"What happened?"

"I told you — he hasn't changed at all, oh you mean what happened at work. Well, let me see, I saw Phillips again and he, I can't remem — um talk about it, you know my job. Another council meeting."

She made a little unh huh laugh and didn't say anything. She watched him.

She liked him. He saw her looking.

It wasn't because of the dream he couldn't remember, nor was it because he had had a dream. Everybody dreams. But it was because of the feeling of seeing him again, and that night having a dream, as if he was in — as if he was a dream. She lies too.

I'm being irrational, he thought. What's going on?

The rush of memories that came with it, and he hadn't known him that well — they'd gone to different churches, and hung out in different circles, yet he was memorable, even then. Remember? Seventeen, in high school, his parents had been out of town, the two boys had gotten drunk on his Dad's gin, and — then, in that delightful, dazzling laughter that boy had drunk *his* mother's perfume! staggered across her room — his parents' bedroom! leaned against the wallpapered wall, and not trying very hard to control himself, laughed —

"I *love* this bedroom!"

Couldn't stop laughing! What did it mean?

Well, Mom said he was crazy, so did Dad, but did Dad care? So the incident faded into the future, graduation, college, and the two young men not seeing each other except at home on Christmas, and then during the fighting in Europe. The corporate executive had been an officer, a Captain, while his old, somehow curious friend but he didn't want to think about that curious friend but couldn't forget that strange chance meeting in the bar in Paris. He had been with fellow officers, had gone to the men's room, and the uniformed figure next to him, with the imprint of Staff Sergeant's stripes — the stripes removed — on the arm, the man was yet — confirmed as their eyes met in the mirror above the urinals.

"It's a small world," the old friend had smiled.

The Captain was embarrassed, and made sure to leave before the other man did, although, as always, in a way he didn't want to. But he did.

98

They'd zipped up, did not shake hands and facing each other said hello.

"Don't be afraid, Captain," smiled the ex-Sergeant. "I won't embarrass you. I'm glad to see you. You look good."

"But why — why the — ?" the Captain pointed to the imprint of stripes.

"I went AWOL. I've been in prison."

"This is war," said the Captain. "You know regulations."

The ex-Sergeant laughed — ah, a hint of that old laugh! — "Yes, Captain. I know the regulations. I broke them. Conscious, and sober when I did so. Go on back to your friends. I'll wait here. I saw you out there — go, join 'em."

"I don't understand. Are you on the run?"

"I rejoin my company tomorrow."

"But, I — don't understand. I mean — "

"Must you understand? Why? and how and where and when? Come, old friend, don't ask."

The Captain was stunned, the eyes of the other gazed beyond him, in sadness, yet warmth, and the pale patch where stripes had been held a terrible mystery.

"But how will you — what did you — ?"

"Let it be."

The two men looked at each other, and the ex-Sergeant smiled, watching the Captain leave.

Yet standing at the bar with his fellow officers the Captain saw the ex-Sergeant leave the men's room, cross the crowded smoky room to a table, and sit next to a French girl, makeup and all, a girl, not seventeen, no doubt a whore, but who *took the hands of that man into hers* and as envy, guilt and grief smashed through the Captain's heart, he froze, as his friend folded his hands over the girl's hands, and lowered his head until his forehead rested on their clasped hands, and he wept, while the Captain watched.

Not because of the dream he couldn't remember, having just seen him and then in dreaming, but sitting in his chair, in his office, staring at the opposite wall. His children were married with children of their own, he loved his wife, their house was beautiful, he had a good job, he had everything and, although he was, he knew, perhaps too controlled, too unspoken and cautious, in his way he was a warm and understanding man. He was, in his own dictionary, the definition of a good man accepting responsibilities.

I'm being defensive, he thought. I must be guilty. But why?

Hearing laughter.

But wasn't part of growing up to lose that laugh? Wasn't a man supposed to be a Man. To be a *Man* — and give up childish ways?

"What are you doing these days?" he had asked. Standing on the sidewalk, where they had met. His friend glanced at a passing woman and said he was surviving.

"Doing what?"

The other man looked at him, but didn't speak, and the corporate executive was baffled, thus silent, and in the noon rush of traffic the two men stood, looking at each other.

The executive in his suit and tie and the other in t-shirt, chinos and sneaks. Both men healthy, in the April month.

"How's Mary Ann?"

The corporate executive said, "Fine." Just fine.

"Good. From what I hear, and read in the papers, you're all okay, right?"

"Yes, yes, we're all fine."

"Unspoken as ever."

"Yes."

"May I tell you something?"

"Not before you tell me how you live."

"I'm a musician. I play trumpet, and I'm in love again."

"Are you in — a band, or — "

That laugh!

"Well I sit in once in a while. But no, I compose. I'm writing a symphony."

"Do you have any luck?"

"I got the NEA last year."

"How do you pay your bills?"

"I paint apartments, do carpentry, plumbing — "

"Would you like me to — not to offend you, I mean — but, would you like a job? Perhaps I — "

"No, not yet, but thanks. I mean it. May I tell you something?"

The corporate executive smiled, and as a ray of sunlight twinkles on Atlantic waves, in a flash the composer saw the face of a boy before him.

"Yes," the corporate executive said. His heart — !

"Good," said the other. "You know, I've always loved you. I didn't know you very well way back then, but — maybe you knew, in your heart. We liked being together, remember? I don't mean to make you self-conscious."

"No, you're right. I do remember. I've thought of you."

"I envied you, wishing I had your control, and—your quiet. I still envy you. When I see your name in print, your picture in the papers, I don't envy your success, I envy what it is that you are. Did you know that since your dad died, I've kept in touch with your mom? A card once in a while. She likes that. I once wished she were mine."

"She's told me you've written. It's very thoughtful, of you," but the corporate executive was shaken. The other was speaking.

"Your mom is exceptional, though she writes little in return, her few words convey much more. You have no idea how much of her you are. I envy that, more than I know, and what has made you a success has made me—and will make me—at center a failure as a composer. I could use your sureness, your ambition, and level head."

"I'm beginning to be exasperated," said the corporate executive, "because I don't altogether understand."

"Must you understand everything?"

"You're saying I'm like my mother, and you'd like that influence, is that it?"

"Yes," the composer smiled, putting his hand on his friend's shoulder—"you're the best tonic in the world for a romantic like me."

"All right, I can see that. I have to get back to work."

"And I to meet my love for lunch. One question?"

"One."

"Do you know who was in love with you in high school?"

The confusion on the other's face was visible.

"No," he said.

"Remember Shirley Dahl?"

The executive's lips parted, his eyes widened, and following a quiet sigh, said he did indeed remember Shirley Dahl, but he didn't, hadn't known, how—why? and how come he—how did the other man know?

"She wrote me."

"She wrote you!"

That delightful laugh! And—his ears *rang.*

Shirley too had been shy, but ambitious, she too had become a success, had married, had children—she too made the papers—in Dallas, and a few years ago, having seen the notice of his concert there, she had attended and since then kept in touch.

Thus the corporate executive was having a difficult day, sitting at his desk, and staring across the room, for without warning he was in

101

study hall, sitting next to Shirley Dahl, who was so shy and beautiful he—

closed his eyes, put his elbows on his desk and his face in his hands, bit his lips, and—his heart danced! *She had loved him!* and, after a clap on his back, his childhood friend, still laughing to be sure—*just as he was*—just as they *both* were! He hadn't laughed like that since—since—since they, they were boys.

And walking away, his friend had called—"My regards to Mary Ann, please. Say hello!"

"I will by all means," returned the corporate executive.

Which he did. Oh yes, in his corporate executive way, the adult, fifty-three year old grandfather of three, father of two and husband of one—had given his old friend's regards to his wife Mary Ann, but Mary Ann had—thought something was different. Her controlled and quiet husband was a little too warm, in fact a little too happy? There must be a woman.

True, but how could he tell her?

Should he?

Shirley Dahl.

Such amusement!

He raised his head and smiled, and though there was a bright and rather winsome look in his eyes, it was the face of the corporate executive coming to a decision, which was visible, yet slow appearing, while I stood across the room, leaning against the wall. He didn't see me, but he heard me—

Why not tell her? She'll like it. Maybe she'll hand *you* a surprise.

The executive's face cleared.

"That's it!" he said, out loud. "She *will* like it!"

Which was true. For—in fact—not only did Mary Ann like it, she was delighted, and confessed that she had been in love with a football star who, it turned out years later, she had met at that party in San Francisco, who—

"So that was the guy so sweet on you!" exclaimed her husband. "On *our* anniversary!"

"He was still in love with me, too," she smiled, in reply. "I'd like to meet your composer friend. What's his name again? Pan?" she chuckled. "Why don't you invite him up for a drink?" A novelty.

"I am not much of a man with words," smiled her husband, "but you in love with that football player and he in love with you, and me in love with Shirley Dahl, and she in love with me, isn't that enough as it is?"

"You're right. Why did you tell me?"

"I don't know—I think I thought of it—I thought I should. At work today." He paused. "On a hunch. What's that about Pan?"

Suburban talk. But she had, he remembered, been an English major in college, so Pan, the word, came natural to her. Therefore, in his corporate executive's follow-through style, to satisfy her curiosity, he telephoned Pan, and invited him up for drinks, Sunday. Pan declined—a rehearsal, which startled the executive, and a little hurt him, but upon telling Mary Ann the bad news he discovered she wasn't interested anymore, as she had found another diversion, so when, later that year Pan sent them two tickets for the performance of his symphony, they didn't go, which didn't surprise Pan in the least, although he was a little hurt, he wanted him to hear his music, for no matter what the corporate executive would think, the boy would know.

The Answer

After John R. Tunis
— for Helen Maldovan

HE TOOK HIS STANCE under the lights. The machine shot the ball, he swung, and smacked a double into the net.

On the next mechanical pitch he hit a single up what would be the middle.

He missed the next pitch, and cursed.

"Enjoy taking out your aggressions?" she asked, from outside the cage.

"We've been through this before," he said, perspiring.

"If you hit this well during the games," she said, knowing she was making him angry — he was in a slump — "you wouldn't need this."

"I don't need it, I want it."

He hit the next pitch down the nowhere line, which would have gone deep into the left field corner, and had a man been on first the run would have scored. It would have been a double, and if the left fielder had made one false move, a triple.

His base-running style was like that. He rounded first as he rounded second around third: the next base always in his eye and mind, with home the big one ever waiting. He was a natural, hardboiled, fast-handed, first rate pro, and he hit the next pitch to an invisible short-stop for a sure out.

He met the next pitch direct, and sent it into what would have been left center for a classic two base hit. She said,

"That was the best yet."

He agreed, dug in, and hit the next and last machine pitch into the air nowhere, and had there been a center fielder, it would have been an easy out.

"Do you want to hit some more?" she asked.

"No," he said. "I'm sick of you."

"Would you love me if I was a tennis star?"

"I'd hate your Goddamned guts no matter what you were."

"But—"

"Don't give me that but shit. We've been through this. I can't help it. I hit .298 last year and you know what I hit the year before, so you know how I feel. This is my third year and my third slump. They've been good to me so far, as they were last year and the year before. I'll get back somehow. Leave me alone."

She was coy. "I didn't know you could talk so much."

He walked out of the cage, holding his bat, and they walked toward the car.

She was being cruel, and she knew it. A guy in a slump in the baseball circus is a guy gone crazy, and a ballplayer so talented as her husband in this slump made life impossible. It was the same with pitchers on a long losing streak, their wives went through hell, so, she told herself, she should know better. But she too was angry, because it was, all of it, unfair, even though she married into it, and her battle against her self-pity was overwhelming. She wasn't, in truth, introspective, nor was he, but each had an at-bottom sensibility, and together they had their smarts. This was their world, a major league reality, and the odds against him being a star were incomprehensible, too remote for them to think of, and in such demanding draining competition, they did their best to take the games one by one, yet in this slump even his remote starship faded. The grim statistics made actuality crackle.

All he knew by heart and nature, and developed discipline, was baseball, and as they both knew, as the team knew, as ballplayers know, even though he was a dependable, fast-handed, fast thinking second baseman, he would be finished, if he was lucky, in so few years that the children, Nick six and Becky seven, young as they were, were already showing stress signs.

At twenty-seven, she twenty-eight, he — or they — had been in the majors two years. This was his third. It had taken him four years, after college — a B.A. in Business Administration.

Two years ago he had come within a handful of votes of making Rookie of the Year, and the reason he didn't wasn't reported in all the papers, but anybody who knew baseball knew his year's end .296 batting average had come from .251 in the second week in August, and helped bring his team into 4th place from 7th, finishing, in a tight race, six and a half games out.

Then, in July of last year he had gone into a five week slump, and was, he felt, responsible for his team's losing second place, although he had gotten hot — again in August, and from a .235 average, ended hitting .298. Fifth in the RBI column, seventh in hits. Second in doubles. These second year statistics were impressive, but the papers had their usual fun. A hot weather hitter. Lucky he didn't make Rookie of the Year because he'd be where the guy who did make it was — hitting .170, etc., yet this second baseman, his wife and their children were bitter, frustrated, confused and helpless. They read the papers every day, and in this, his third year, they read about him. Last year he had gone almost crazy, became more superstitious, choked up an inch on his bat, shortened his stance, and kept remembering what Clemente had said — "All I want is a clean base hit" — that beery July, that became the August and September champagne days, singles stretched into doubles, stealing third, and the daring race to home on shallow outfield flies, as the crowd went wild.

But this season — this was the first week of June, and the anxiety at home was dreadful. She was so neutralized by her involvement in his slump it was difficult for her to separate her feelings — his slump and confusion as against the real tasks at hand. She didn't know what to do, nor did he, and the children were as if stunned by parental self-control over fury and conflict, and in the face of it, in the family as a whole, a pattern of violence was beginning to form.

That night, after they'd driven away from the suburban batting cage, they drove in silence, reflecting in a scarlet gloom. It had been a night game, and with men on first and second, two down, bottom of the ninth, he had looked at the third strike, and they lost it by one.

He was, he felt, in a trance, or suspension. He seemed fated, and in the literal storm of irrationality he didn't know what to do. In the locker room he had fought hard, but then had wept, changed clothes without showering and left the stadium. The other ballplayers wore masks of unconcern, for they might be next. Except Jake, their catcher, who watched with concern as his second baseman changed clothes, then walked out.

The team's wives, who had sat with his wife, comforted her, for she too had wept. Those wives knew. You bet they knew. The team knew, the owners, the reporters — everybody inside knew, although the knowing was irrelevant, because the situation was impossible. From out of nowhere Fate had made a gesture, and one man's life became a nightmare. He'd had one hit in his last seventeen games, and that a blooper. He was hitting .229.

Jake was coming out of a brief slump, thank God, but to the man who followed Jake in the batting order — Jake hit 4th — it was doomsday, and with Jake on first, and their center fielder on second, he had taken that third strike. The manager had shaken up the batting order as it was, and this could not go on.

What is it? he asked, as he drove.

And the fans, those wonderful fans, who had cheered, and cheered, and cheered to make the stadium rock had, on that third strike booed, and booed some more before they all went home.

Meanwhile the papers were having fun, one columnist saying, regarding the second baseman's slump, August was looking like the discovery of DNA as seen from the 16th Century. Others said other things (bench him).

His wife sat beside him in the car, tightlipped, hurt, and in such fury and chaos she looked like a smooth but hollow white statue, her pretty face drawn and ashen.

He couldn't get the image of himself taking that third strike out of his mind. He had as if seen the pitch from a distant place, and the ball, taking its graceful sliding curve down over the outside corner, on the knees, seemed an alien object. But *why?* he asked. *Why?* That wasn't me. I *never* take the third one. Never! What is it?

He felt he was floating, and within himself he was terrified. After tonight's game— .226, his team was in fourth place, percentage points from fifth, four games out of third, six from second, and nine from first. True, he had turned over an unassisted double play which had, it appeared, saved the game, but they needed his bat—life needs blood.

"Let me drive," she said.

He pulled over, stopped the car, and they changed places.

"Why don't you see the team shrink again?" she asked. She despised shrinks. They took him away from her.

"It won't work," he murmured. "It's up to me. Me alone. I've got to do it. There aren't any answers because the questions fuck them up. I'm going crazy—*why* is it? Why? I'm a *good* hitter!"

She wiped her eyes and drove with care, God how unfair it was. Twenty-seven years old—so young, yet so sophisticated it became a paradox—all unfair! *And so brutal.* He hung his head, and slumped forward, like a boy.

Every single thing they did, had, knew, felt, wanted, and needed— or owned, owed, loved and avoided or took for granted—was on his shoulders. Their world was up to him, and his guilt, anxiety, sense of helplessness, frustration, fear, confusion and fury threw their world in to frenzy. The word *hit* had implications the children were beginning to act out.

When he had taken that third strike, her heart had stopped.

She pulled into the parking lot of an all night diner, braked, cut the engine, turned to him and said,

"What's it going to be, August or Business Administration? I want an answer."

"I don't know," he mumbled. "I'm in a dream."

"Well," she said, keeping control. "I'm not, although what I'm witnessing, and feeling, seems like it, *I* am not in a dream, nor are our children."

But — as he put his arms on the dash and his head on his arms — in a flash of higher consciousness, she saw him, and in him, a terrible vision of a broken boy, close to the edge, who might go over, helpless. She stared at him, and suddenly —

Fight him. Fight him!

"Get out of the car," she said. "Come on, get out of the car."

He looked at her in disbelief.

"Get *out* of the car," she repeated, opening her door, and getting out. He was startled, and baffled, but he got out, and they walked around until they faced each other in the beam of headlights.

In fear, fury, and a morality mix, she gathered her strength —

"If you don't hit me first I'm going to hit you."

She counted out loud to three, and slapped him, surprising him as he took a couple of steps backward, but she followed, counted to three again, and with flashing eyes and clenched fist in an overhand swing socked him square in the teeth. His lip split, and began to bleed — he backed away, hands out, still surprised, and confused as she advanced again counting to three, and swung. But he caught her arm and they stood, locked, but she struggled, and bit his left forearm with all her power, he cried out, released her, ducked under her right swing and in quick rage and his eyes blazing pasted her cheek with a left jab and her jaw with a hard right cross. She stumbled backwards, and fell, but when he picked her up she hit him in the eye and he delivered a shot from his shoulder which sent her reeling, and she fell — down, and almost out.

He bent over her, as she lay on the asphalt parking lot. He smiled an angry smile, his lips and teeth bloody, and dripping on her cheek, he asked,

"Want some more?"

"No." She tilted her head to avoid his blood and to spit out her own, saying, "But thanks anyway, you bastard."

Her upper lip was split and bleeding, and the tip of her left eyetooth was somewhere on the asphalt. He helped her up. She put her arm around him, and as they walked, she asked if he would drive, as she didn't feel very well.

He helped her into the car, walked around, got in the driver's seat, they wiped each other's blood off, with his handkerchief, and Kleenex from the glove compartment, blotting blood from their clothes, and as she held his hanky to her mouth and they pulled out onto the highway again, she said,

"Jesus. I didn't know you could hit like that."

In the innocent pun dawning, they began to laugh, but when the pun turned into irony, they laughed harder.

"I'm pulling over," he laughed. "I can't drive!"

The car angled onto the shoulder of the highway, and they sat in the front seat laughing out of control, bleeding anew, until they were exhausted, and he drove home, thanked and paid the astonished babysitter, and after washing up, applying iodine, bandaids and ice packs, they sat at the kitchen table and each drank a cold beer through straws, looking at each other. They held hands across the table. Then went to bed and fell asleep in an embrace, wiped out, but before he went altogether unconscious, he realized his bloodstream had changed. His body felt fluid and warm.

She had a smile on her face. His sleep was pure, and deep.

The next day was predictable.

He knelt in the on-deck circle, in the bottom of their first, and watched Jake slash a single into right, advancing their third baseman to third. One out, one run was in. The man in the on-deck circle rose to his feet, took a couple of swings, tossed the ring-weight away, walked to the plate — not glancing at his wife in the stands. Their dentist had sanded her eyetooth down, her upper lip was swollen and bandaged. The other wives were embarrassed, staring out at the field, and the game under the lights, not seeing much of either, nor not quite knowing what to say. She was a fright, in her hope.

What was in his mind, or in himself, he didn't know, or care about, but with a black eye, split lip, bruised cheekbone, aching right hand, and left forearm bright with teethmarks — which the team enjoyed no end — he dug in the box motioning to the umpire to allow it, which the ump acknowledged, himself a little startled, watching that battered ballplayer dig in, take a couple of swings, and as the umpire nodded to the pitcher, as from a vast and remote section of the galaxy, an alien force invaded the batter, and as the pitcher, glancing at the men on base, went into the stretch, the man he saw at the plate seemed a different man, whose eyes glowed, with tiny looping nuclear crystals at center, something demonic in that bruised face, something lethal in that batter's stance, something not quite explainable, but yet quite clear, for what followed in the rest of the game, as well as that season, I mean what that man did with that bat, and his glove, made an exact

110

transition to the glory of July in the next year, as the record books tell us. Jake again started for the National League All-Star team. His buddy was number two choice at second (Joe Morgan started).

Number two stood in the dugout, face a mask, he felt the thrill, relaxed and confident — .302 batting average last year — watching a blonde rock star walk to the microphone at home plate, and begin to sing the Star Spangled Banner. Jake stood on the steps of the dugout, catcher's gear on, ballcap held over his heart. The song rose, he looked at his feet, not seeing anything, but beginning to hear the ballpark turn in on the jewel of itself, suspended between fifty thousand people and himself, that song, and as it went toward crescendo, space narrowed to a margin he knew by heart, a margin which gave him peace of mind, and in a cresting crashing wave of sound the anthem was over. The park winked back to its stoic limits. The game was on.

In the fifth inning he hit for Morgan, lined deep into left center for an out, and in the next inning, the sixth, score tied two all, with one out, the fastest base runner in the American League reached first on a bunt, and on the second pitch to the right-handed hitter, the runner broke for second, the batter swung to protect his runner and Jake in one fluid motion followed the swing of the bat with a single throw to the perfect running action of his second baseman, the sweeping tag was made, the runner was out, and as the fans cheered, the second baseman, professional face without expression, snapped the ball to his shortstop who zipped it to their third baseman, and thus the ball returned to the pitcher. The second baseman resumed his position, wanting, above all things, that the ball be hit to him. His wife was in the stands, sitting beside Jake's wife, both women happy, and pretty, their children beside them.

"They're sensational."

"They are," the second baseman's wife agreed. "Jake's a genius. He knew that guy was going."

"So did your husband," Jake's wife smiled, and the two women gazed at each other, their eyes warm, as the hitter sent a lazy fly ball high above the brilliant green grass of the field, the small white sphere reached the peak of its arc, and below a deep blue and black moonlit sky, fell for the third out into the waiting glove of the National League's left fielder as millions round the world watched, either on satellite or domestic television, or saw it in their ear's eye over radio, bringing childhood's vividness back again, or making childhood in fact that much more vivid. It went to American businessmen and GIs by tv or radio everywhere in the world — to certain interested parties in England — it

111

swept through Mexico, Puerto Rico and to Fidel Castro himself, as well as Hawaii, Australia, the Phillipines, to Korea, Alaska, to the baseball island of Japan, and to all guys and women of all races at bars across the U.S. and Canada, to speeding trains, to planes midflight, and to astronauts among the stars — a small, old woman in a rocking chair, bright eyes glued to the tv screen as Jake walked to bat in the living room of her small, clean woodframe house, on the outskirts of Sweetwater, Oklahoma, as she whispered *Come on Jake, come on boy*, and rubbed her hands as she smiled.

The Secret Circle

—for Ed Kane

AFTER HE HAD GONE to his bank he realized he had a hangover, so he straightened his dark glasses, and as it was warm, he unbuttoned his raincoat, and walked down the street to the bar with the red door.

Another new place wanting to look old. Dark ceiling beams and overhead wagon-wheel light fixtures. Prints of old New York lined the wall opposite the bar. But rising up from behind the bar, from the floor to ceiling, stood a wood structure with many cabinets with glass doors surrounded in a geometric whole by inset mirrors next to small carved gargoyles, hidden cabinets, cubbyholes and shelves, at the center of which complete structure, one long mirror at eye level reflected the opposite wall and the prints as well as the seated or standing customers at the bar. On shelves at the foot of this long mirror, rows of full and not so full bottles twinkled in the rather dim light. The whole structure ran the length of the bar, and as it was forty or more feet long, the sight was impressive.

At the center of the bar, beer taps, and on top of two long wooden handles that drew Schlitz beer, were silver worlds, and perched atop each world, a silver statue of Psyche knelt, gazing, in her prim way, down, stripped to the waist. To draw the beer the bartender should have put his hand or fingers around her metal breasts, but he used his first two fingers on her knees, and it occurred to the man in the dark glasses, fresh but shaky from his bank, that the Schlitz's Psyche embarrassed the bartender.

The man in dark glasses ordered a drink, got it, paid for it, and in a bit of a tremble, sipped it. Because the afternoon was so sunny, and light flowed through the front window, he kept his dark glasses on, but glanced around out of habit to see if anyone he knew was there. In the rear dining area the lights were low, as usual, and it was dark, scattered couples finished their lunches. No familiar faces. The front of the place was quiet, the mid-week afternoon in its usual routine — a wealthy, myopic, plump and rather owlish man sat at his usual table

113

up front with his face buried in the morning paper, and a young man and his girlfriend sat at the bar near the door, drank Bud in bottles, and talked.

A neighborhood building super drank a stein of Schlitz near the beer taps.

Yet, in a curious placement, or perhaps arrangement in the space between the rear of the restaurant and the front, straight across the floor from the man in dark glasses, an odd-looking man around thirty-five seeming fifty, sat at a table with his daughter. It was clear she was his daughter for she looked very much like him, although she was not yet ten.

As in a play the odd-looking man rose to his feet, finished his coffee, walked across the floor to the telephone booth, shut himself in, the light went on and the man in dark glasses saw a shadow dialing, eyes behind dark glasses swung back to the girl, and fixed.

She had inherited the best of her father's features, for he was a character out of Hardy, rather boorish looking, thickset in face, neck and figure, a peasant type and brooding over it. The kind of man who, upon hearing something he didn't want to hear, yet knew it was important to the speaker, might pull his lips down in soft distaste, as in a low pucker. His lips were thick, nose unformed, his eyes small, dark, and cautious. His hair was thick, the color of the shag that Holmes used to smoke, and hung in limpid spikes on his temples, and down over his low forehead. His face was lined and pockmarked. He was wearing a tobacco brown corduroy jacket, blue chambray shirt, red plaid cotton tie, tan slacks, and dark brown boots to match the rest.

But in his daughter's face—she was around seven or eight—his features had not developed, which, thought the man in dark glasses, gave her a pretty gloomy future, for she looked so like her father at this point, if mother didn't show up soon, how, in short, would she look when she was twenty?

The conjecture depressed him, so he rejected it, knowing how often children, even very young children, could be photocopies of either parent, and during or just after puberty, as if overnight turn into themselves and look no more like mom or dad than the chief of police.

But this little girl looked like her father in an eerie way, that while mirroring him, in seeing her, gave father a reflected feminine look, his boorish expression held a soft, mother-like comprehension, to her in her light blue frock, white socks and glossy blackstrapped shoes, his small dark eyes big in her face, and as she hadn't learned to veil them, her eyes had his strength, and because of his evident character, her eyes were candid. Sad to think how many children hold that honest look —

114

until they get smart. See how much is lost in growing up.

Her dark brown hair, held in place by barrettes, curved forward to tips, and as her skin was clear and her nose the famous button, she looked cute. She had his lips, but without the pucker, and on her they were the cherry red of childhood, yet in his thickness — not yet altogether defined — one saw a faint male sensuality.

The man in dark glasses finished his drink, which had tasted bitter, but being hungover in an upswing, he ordered another and turned away from the girl at the table waiting for her father to finish his telephone call. He adjusted his dark glasses — he was perspiring so they slipped down his nose — and staring into his fresh drink he fell into his afternoon thoughts, which centered around the steady question: how long was the money going to last?

In this as in other ways, he was like other men, but in another way, not in the least. He was of average height, rather pale with thin black hair and in features resembled men the world over.

But he was uneasy, because he'd done something that had taken him out of his orbit, and he'd gotten himself into a mess. None of it was his fault, either! He wasn't a writer! Yet one morning a couple of years ago he had awakened, sat up in bed, and — perhaps because of the dream he'd just had — in terms of sound as clear as a bell, complete from the beginning right out of the blue, he saw a short story.

He phoned in sick to his boss, and on that day wrote the story, the first draft was excellent — he knew what a bad first draft meant — the next day called in sick again, typed the final clean copy, and through a guy he knew got an agent who sold the story for three thousand, and, based on that success, and feeling ambitious, he quit his job, did the first fifty pages of a detective novel, and with an accompanying outline, gave it to the agent who sold it to a publisher for ten thousand, five down and five on the delivery of the manuscript.

Since then, which was causing him increasing anxiety, in the lucid realization that he was not a writer, he had done nothing with the book, the money was long gone, and just before he had begun looking for another job — he was a copywriter — fate, in the teeth of that doomsday chore, gave him a break via a guy he didn't quite like but who was an interesting storyteller at the bar as well as at the racetrack, for he couldn't stop telling stories, but who knew, so most agreed, about horses, so as the man in dark glasses, on his way out of town to visit a lady friend in the country for the weekend, heard something much like a voce say: *e, d, f,* in his ear, and wondering what that meant, but remembering Chester Himes, on a hunch he phoned his story-telling friend who laughed and said it's a long shot, but put eighteen on the trifecta at OTB, which he did, and won the triple for fifteen hundred dollars, and following his weekend in the country, returned to town, picked up his money, paid his next month's rent, plus several debts, and put five hundred in his bank, which gave him six hundred and fifty less the twenty he was spending at the bar, how long would six hundred and thirty last, and what was he going to do about his novel? He didn't like to think of the days and nights he'd worked at it, with such terrible results he wished he'd never begun it, and of course the news from his agent reminding him that he had signed a contract, the publisher was getting angry and using words like deadline which if not met, said publisher will demand return of the five grand, which meant — although he had had a lot of fun during the last two years, having had a couple of thousand before he sold the story, not to mention the book, or the luck at the tracks, and the freelance copywriting jobs, something had to happen, and as he again adjusted his dark glasses, stared into his drink, stirred it, and sipped, he had to get busy, his lies were getting thin, and as he was a poor liar anyway —

He had a problem.

But while he was no different than other men, there was one way he was unique.

Had his anxiety, worry and apprehension been that of a creative man, he might have realized that his key to the completion of his novel, although not being easy, was, in one exact sense clear. Details were easy, so while he lacked imagination, given an idea could, with amazing authority, grasp, and render it in writing. He was excellent at his job, a job which he said he hated but in secret enjoyed. And because he was honest with himself, his awareness of his talent gave him the vision of his limitations. He *used* ideas. Therefore, in this spot he was in, his need for a plot was enormous — beyond his reach! He had based his story on an unknown story by De Maupassant, then he had based his novel on his story, and while keeping the original De Maupassant intact, he had been able to base his outline in fine detail. All this he remembered because he had a good memory, but also because it was unforgettable. No matter how often he thought of it, he remembered the whole thing! as fresh as it had occurred, yet he hadn't had a hand in it! All he'd done was do it!

There he was, at a dull party while the woman he'd been with talked with people he didn't know, and while making himself a drink in the kitchen he saw, on the windowsill a book, and out of curiosity picked it up. 200 hundred short stories of De Maupassant published by Walter

Black in 1922, and for the hell of it, he opened the book, flipped through it, and around halfway saw a title, and leaning against the sink sipping his drink, read the story, put the book down in shock, made another drink, and felt something turn, like a small wheel, in the back of his mind: stopped, click. He wasn't much of a talker, so didn't talk about it, and the days, weeks and months went by, he went to work, came home, had dates, lived his rather normal bachelor's life, except — that special morning when he had awakened, and having had a dream of De Maupassant, saw the complete story he would write, and all the rest had followed. While realizing he was working variants, he took that French tiger, tooth, tail and hide, which is how he was able to finish his outline — well detailed, good brief description, the first fifty pages solid, but it was clear that if all of it was 95% Maupassant it could be called a downright — well, never mind, publishers didn't give a damn where it came from, but the main trouble was, not that they would realize he had stolen it, or a possible copyright hassle — he felt a tug at his raincoat, and he turned, looked down, surprised, seeing the upturned face of the little girl, eyes grave on his eyes, dark glasses notwithstanding, as his thoughts concluded: the main trouble was, details and description aside, not to mention lack of inspiration, he could not get a couple of hundred more pages out of an outline based on De Maupassant's six.

The girl didn't smile. She held up a small straw, not one of the long drinking kind, he saw she wanted a favor, looking him square in the eyes, right through his glasses, and saying something so strange, so weird, he doubted his ears, and after having thought those dreadful thoughts about his book, he doubted his ears all the more, so he bent down, thinking his face must be looking strange, too, and in that sort of disbelief, he said,

"What?"

"Make an O!"

Holding the straw up to him.

He didn't know what to do. But he put his drink on the bar, and looked down at her as she shook the straw up at him for him to take, which he did. It was thin, plastic, with a miniature candystripe, meant to stir drinks, not to drink through, although people did, tourists in the drinking world.

"You want an O out of this?"

"Yes."

"But listen," he said, explaining the useless detail, "it's too small, too thin, and it's plastic. It's stiff, won't bend. I can't do it," he shrugged.

117

"I'm sorry."

She thought about that as he held it, both looking at it, as he thought aw well hell, a little girl.

"Okay, I'll try."

He took off his dark glasses, his bloodshot eyes not mattering to her, nor his trembling fingers: she knew what she wanted.

Therefore, in the glare from the front window (and no reading glasses!), with his thumbnail he made a tiny dent in one end of the straw, pinched that end together, and without success tried to bend the straw into a circle, but instead achieved a triangle, so he inserted the pinched end into the other open end, forcing the pinched end in further until it stuck. He gave it to her, pleased with himself, thinking the good little girl would thank him, but no. In silence he put his dark glasses back on as she looked at the triangle.

"It's a triangle," she said.

But it was supposed to be a circle.

Yet she played with it, turning it from side to side as he glanced at the telephone booth, seeing the shadow still talking, so he turned to the bar and sipped his drink wondering if her parents were divorced.

He lit a cigarette which tasted bad, and while he considered putting it out, she tugged on his raincoat again.

The triangle had fallen onto the floor. She looked up at him, he looked down at her, and then at the triangle. It lay near the foot of the empty barstool next to him, and without reading his mind (not needing to), she picked up the triangle in an obedient albeit indifferent way, held it in her hands looking at it, and then looked up to him. Then at the seat of the empty barstool, which was just about level with her eyes.

The barstools weren't the usual kind, these were high hardwood swivel chairs with curved backs and arms attached to the seats by spokes, and as on each there were some six spokes, when she placed the triangle down in the space between the first two spokes, she said that was her house, and moving to her left, placing the triangle between the second and third spokes, said this was her neighbor's house, her eyes were on her triangle, and placing the triangle between the third and fourth spokes announced that this was her other neighbor's house, setting it between fourth and fifth spokes — this was her church, following the curve of the spokes around as she went, speaking while he puffed on his cigarette, finished his drink, licked his lips the cigarette tasted better, and catching the bartender's eye, ordered another drink, glanced at the shadow in the telephone booth and wondered who the girl's father

118

was talking to, and why he was taking so long.

But the girl, then wanting the man in dark glasses' attention, had seen him look at the telephone booth, and something crossed her face so fast he couldn't identify it, but the flicker held something, was it sadness? anger — irritation? Yet he thought he saw something inevitable which sent a chill up his spine, but she lowered her head having made sure he had seen her, and she continued to play her game as he sipped his drink and smoked his cigarette keeping an eye on her, he aware of her and she of him.

He didn't know anything about children except once he had been a child. Those memories, if revealed, would be vivid in detail, but lacking in continuity (to him), and although he was a sensible as well as sensitive man, in an actual sense things occurred to him without thought — words, action — they didn't evolve.

She saw he was preoccupied in a way that wasn't useful to her, although he was decent enough to keep an eye on her, so it was with a condescending boredom that she returned to the table where she and her father had been, she sat down and played with her triangle. Her eyes, as quick as his — they both saw other small straws beside glasses and plates and silverware on cloth placemats and within himself he smiled as she picked up a straw, and rising from the table, crossed the floor to him, and told him to make another.

He did.

The second triangle.

As he held it she gave him the first, returned to the table and came back with another straw, but instead of giving it to him, she tried, as he watched her which she intended, to tie the straw into a knot, which she couldn't, for it sprang back into its former shape, and getting interested in this detail, the man in dark glasses forgot his hangover, and by pulling the straw between his right thumbnail and index fingernail, flattened it, and it seemed that the sides had split, but not so, for he inserted it through both triangles, and as before joined the flat straw, thus joining the triangles together, which was what she wanted and she was delighted. They grinned. Pretty great! She held up the two joined triangles like a couple of chimes, and in a no-sound, jiggled them, her eyes bright, and a smile on her strong, pretty face.

"Not bad, eh?" he said.

"Good!" she cried.

He finished his drink and ordered another — the bartender, a company man, made small drinks — lit a cigarette which tasted better but put it out, he was smoking too much. He had his back to the girl, and was—astonished!

She had, behind his back, put her left foot up on the footrest of the empty barstool, grabbed his right sleeve, and before he knew what had happened she had swung her right foot up onto the seat, put her left hand on the back of the swivel chair, to steady it, and holding him for support with her right, quick! was up, standing on the seat, and looking down at him, eyes triumphant.

He watched, incredulous.

She knelt, in a rather shy fashion, smoothed out her dress and got comfortable, as in position to play jax, and he was unnerved.

She still had her toy, and with a look that might, in the not too distant future, be called wicked, she smiled, as with care and every caution she folded the toy so the two triangles overlapped, while staying intact, and putting the toy in her left hand she cupped her right hand over so he couldn't see, and as he removed his dark glasses, she said—

"You can't look."

He turned away.

"Don't turn away," she demanded. "Stand *here*. But don't look!"

The man, a good deal more than baffled—gaped.

"Close your eyes!"

He closed his eyes.

"Open them!"

He opened them.

Her two fists were out, clenched. Her eyes were marvelous, challenging and astute, as she, keen and cool, ordered him to do the obvious, he did, touching her left fist, and—that got her. Knocked her out! How? How did he know? Talk about a talking expression! And she laughed! How she laughed! But then—her sharp voice:

"Close your eyes!"

Done.

Ah, she was smart, and sly, and brilliant. It took quick thought, and after a consideration of opposites, a realization of a new concept.

He knew she was smart, but this—

"Open!"

He opened his eyes and she had both fists out again, her face radiant and eyes foxy. She had him—she knew it. But this would, she also knew, cap everything, and in his naked world without dark glasses he felt doomed, and the shrewd pleasure in her eyes bid him pause to consider alternatives: if the last trick was with her left hand, would she go to her right, or, to fool him, use her left again? No, she would go to her right because she would know he wouldn't be so foolish to think she'd use her left again, yet his hand trembled as his index finger touched her right fist.

Her face changed, became dead serious, eyes level, while suppressing a wild shout between pressed lips, she shook her head twice. No.

The man without dark glasses looked at the girl and she looked right back. They looked at each other. Her smile made Mata Hari look too too naive, and the way the man who must have the second ace in seven card reaches for his last down card, he touched her left fist.

In a tempest of laughter causing everyone in the restaurant to look, including the bartender, she shrieked, shut her mouth, and froze her face in silence, but on her parted lips the man she faced saw a large and silent NO, eyes dancing. Stunned, he was embarrassed, and furious.

"Where is it!" he yelled, and again people turned, as she reached around behind her, and brought the toy into view, holding it before his eyes. She had tucked it in her belt, in back. She showed him.

"*Here* it was!" she laughed, then dangled it in front of him.

"You got me," he smiled, but in conflict almost blushed, for the bartender was watching him with a this-isn't-a-playground look.

"She got me," the man without dark glasses explained, wondering how she could have gotten that idea so fast, she watched him wondering, enjoying him. He sipped his drink, lit the dead cigarette, and looked out the front window, thinking. She had made a fool of him, and in a not so curious adult way he was jealous, and smart enough to realize his jealousy was real. He had often been fooled like this, and he wondered why. He put on his dark glasses, and looked at her.

She had shifted position on the chair, and held out the toy to him. "Your turn."

He shook his head. "No."

Her eyes questioned, and irritation pursed her lips.

"Your," she said, "turn."

"No," he said, meaning it: "You're too smart for me."

But she had heard that before, he realized, so he decided to add to his honesty.

"I'm not good at games like this," he said. "I can't guess at things. You can. You're good. I'm not. I'm no fun."

Well, that was a joke, and her cynicism, if not outright disgust, made him feel helpless, self-conscious and a bit desperate, as well as sad, angry, and more hungover.

"I'm telling you the truth," he said.

But no. Even the truth didn't work, so he played the game, feeling she was bullying him, but as he had said, which she then discovered,

121

he wasn't any good and he wasn't any fun, so they stopped, and while she figured out what they would do next — in his way he did too — he finished his drink, put out his cigarette, noticed Psyche on top of Schlitz's world and, just this side of her, saw a clean, empty beer stein filled with long drinking straws, at which detail he stared, until the inspiration happened.

He walked down the bar, took a straw from the stein, returned to his place telling her (who watched), to give him the toy and hold out her right hand which she did. He slipped the long straw through the top triangle of the toy, and bending the long straw so it encircled her wrist, he worked one end into the other end, thus making her a bracelet.

In a serious, definite and unexpected sense, she was impressed.

She looked at it, and then at him. She shook her arm, and hand, hard, but the bracelet held, and she looked at the man in dark glasses like Eeyore realizing Piglet's punctured balloon would fit into Pooh's empty honey jar, her eyes wide, in sincere astonishment as her father came out of the telephone booth.

* * *

The scene had changed.

Her father sat at the table drinking hot coffee, and his daughter sat across from him playing with a spoon and a glass, not noticing that the man at the bar in dark glasses and her father were looking at each other, a thinlipped male look.

Her bracelet had broken, it had gotten in her way and caught on a fork, but she had lost interest in it anyway, which disappointed the man at the bar, and having, he felt, been rejected before he had had a chance to become clear about just what had happened, without knowing why, as he hadn't lost interest in the triangles — he'd made them — he walked across to the table, neglected the bracelet, picked up the two joined triangles, and smiled,

"Hi again."

She looked up, returned the smile, but there was something different in it, as well as about her, that he didn't understand, yet wasn't sure she did either, so perhaps to complete — what it was — he tucked the toy in her hair, behind the barrette over her right ear, stepped back,

122

and as father watched with a slight sneer and darker than dark little eyes, and his daughter gazed up at the man in dark glasses, who spoke—

"There. A flower in your hair."

But, like the man who arrived at the formal party in his long underwear, the man in dark glasses realized, in a thunderclap—how stupid he was! She couldn't see what it looked like!

So before her father's eyes, he swept her up in his arms, carried her across the floor, and held her before the long mirror behind the bar.

She liked what she saw, and as he lowered her to the floor, her eyes beamed thanks. She ran to her father.

"Look Daddy! A flower in my hair!"

Daddy nodded, making a slow sarcastic smile. His voice was bitter. "So I see," he said.

"She's very bright," said the man in dark glasses, standing at his place at the bar. "Remarkable comprehension."

Her father snuck a salty smile into a pock-marked cheek, saying, "I know. It's unfortunate."

The other man felt his face flame, and checked his fury. No matter— no matter, the man was her father, and it was none of his business. He adjusted his dark glasses. No matter how he felt, standing there, the relationship they had was theirs. He finished his drink, lit a cigarette, thinking, his part of the afternoon with the girl was over, and yet, as he stood there, smoking and looking out the front window, he ordered another drink, leaned against the bar and—was aware she was looking at him. He turned. She was looking at him, as before, and regardless of dark glasses, their eyes met, but then she turned away, just as he thought *Sorry sweetheart, he's your dad. I'm not.*

So he sighed, turned, put both hands on the edge of the bar, took off his dark glasses, wiped his face with his hanky, folded and returned it to his pocket, put his glasses back on, sipped his drink, smoked his cigarette and felt helpless, frustrated, and angry, thinking—

What kind of rotten bastard *is* that father? after all that went on with me, what's going on between them?

Answer, obvious. They knew each other. No matter anything, or anyone. They knew each other.

He finished his drink, put out his cigarette, and decided to leave, to do the errands he had cashed the check to do, but in a different sense, because the drinks, small as they were, were beginning to affect him, in a sudden bad mood he had an insight which told him things were not yet over, so he ordered another drink, and while taking the first sip, turned, and looked across at her.

123

She had moved. She had pulled her chair over and was sitting so close to her father as to almost be in his lap. Her head and right shoulder were on his left arm, and her face was turned against his chest. Her hands were in her lap. Her father had adjusted himself to make her comfortable.

The man in dark glasses didn't know what to do, but felt he had to do something, and it occurred to him he could say goodbye. He could say it was nice meeting her, or that it had been fun, or — he walked across and knelt beside her, and told her he had to leave because he had errands to do.

"It was nice meeting you," he said.

She shook her head No, although turning a little, one eye looking up at him. The man in dark glasses held his hand out, for hers. No.

"Aren't you going to shake the nice man's hand?" father asked, in brutal sarcasm.

In a slow, reluctant motion she held out a hand. A closed fist, rather, which her friend, the stranger in the dark glasses, in a gentle move, took in his hand, and shook, but her hand was like her, passive, and as he rose, and said goodbye, her hand returned to her lap, and she was motionless.

He returned to the bar, finished his drink in a single motion, hands shaking in anger, left the bartender a tip and walked toward the front door and went outside seeing the busy street through a red filter — through dark glasses with a far darker heart, not sure he knew what had just happened, except that her father's words — "It's unfortunate." — rang in his ears. But — maybe, maybe she was used to it, and knew how to handle the tones in his voice, which had such dynamic effect on strangers but were so familiar to her, and the man in dark glasses walked down the sidewalk in confusion toward a supermarket, not knowing what to think except that it was possible she was angry because nobody could handle her father like she could, the others went away, always, and it always wore her out, so she returned to father, as one returns exhausted to the familiar, after again taking a chance, and again being disappointed.

So as he shopped, not having planned ahead, he tossed things into his plastic hand basket carelessly.

The circle hasn't closed.

He stopped in his tracks before the vegetable section, adjusted his dark glasses and remembered something. He put his basket on top of a stack of crates of lettuce, lit a cigarette and saw it again. Himself, as he had knelt beside the table with his hand out saying goodbye, in fact, he remembered, he had noticed one of the two triangles on the table, crumpled and disconnected, beside the likewise crumpled straw that had been the link, but the second triangle — he recalled in unusual vividness — as he had in truth not shaken her hand, her hand was a fist, he had taken the tip of one of her fingers which she had allowed him to touch, and as he did, his knuckle grazed the tip of a plastic straw, which she had held, clutched in her fist so he couldn't see it, her secret triangular toy memory of him that he'd felt, in the touch of her finger in his tender farewell.

* * *

"So that was it," he told his girlfriend. The next night after supper.

"Sad," she said, pouring coffee. They were in the living room of her apartment. "Parents can be so damned hateful — "

"I think he was jealous of her."

"If she was as bright as you say, that might well be. It's possible."

"I don't know anything about psychology," he said, "but it seemed that way. I don't know. I don't. I don't know anything."

"I don't either," she said. "Except that my dad was a creep."

But somewhere, somehow it made him uncomfortable, and he said so, adding —

"If I was a writer, I'd write a story about it."

She knew the spot he was in regarding his book, therefore didn't say anything, and around six weeks later, he happened to be in the neighborhood of that bar, and feeling good, not hungover, but thirsty, it was hot and humid, he thought he'd stop in for a beer, but as he opened the red door to enter, the strangest thing — a shadow, or a warp in his vision in a stiff and sudden breeze blurred his sight, something of substance, dark, opaque, whirled before him and wouldn't let him through the doorway. There was nothing there, but something wouldn't let him in, like the feel of a forest with no trees in sight, forbidding him entrance, so, puzzled and in a fright, he backed out onto the sidewalk again, the red door swung shut, and he didn't know what to do.

He stood there, in disbelief, breathing with his mouth open. He adjusted his dark glasses, went to the red door, opened it, and — couldn't get in! although inside the bar there were people, finishing up their lunches, the myopic owl-like millionaire's face buried in the morning

125

paper, the neighborhood super having a beer, and the bartender at work serving others while the whirling invisible forest-feel held the man in dark glasses at bay, and as he pushed forward, it shoved him back, onto the sidewalk, and the red door swung shut, the last thing he saw — bewildered and paralyzed in fright, an unoccupied table across the floor from the far end of the bar, with plates, coffee cup, a couple of drinking glasses, and a little girl in a blue frock, white socks, and black-strapped shoes crossing the floor toward a man who stood alone at the bar, with a drink in his hand, and in her hand she held a small plastic straw.

Gently I got him walking again, and as we went down the sidewalk, I said —

'She did like you, and perhaps the best of them all, but each week when she visited her father and he called her mother, he worked out that game — they both did, in fact. We didn't want you to see her, in her act again, for fear of frightening you away, but because we want you to finish your novel — you have to — I gave you a glimpse. You were right, after each performance she was exhausted, yet never failing in her excellence, which is sad, and what he meant when he said unfortunate.

'But although that isn't the story you want to write, it offers the key to the completion of your novel — wait! What's this? A second-hand bookstore! Look! There! That book! Get that book! *The Works of A. Conan Doyle!* This is the volume you want! *The Black Door*, Garden City, New York, copyright 1927, this will complete your novel! This is your full circle, — and her secret! Yes, pick it up, good, turn to page 270! *The Nightmare Room!* That's it!'

The man in dark glasses crossed the sidewalk and looked over the outside display of second hand books on a small table, and seeing one by Doyle, and on what he thought was a hunch, he bought it, took it home, and that night after a date, before he went to bed, he leafed through the book, found a title he liked — *The Nightmare Room* — and after reading it, read it again, then again, and after three stiff drinks and several cigarettes, he fell asleep thinking, woke the next morning, sat bolt upright in bed, his mind clear and sharp, and while drinking black coffee he took notes, made expanded notes on those notes, giving them their indigenous details, and in the early afternoon went to his desk, which was a mess, found his original fifty pages, crossed out the former title with a blue pencil, and wrote above it *The Secret Circle.* His heart was high and a little wild. He realized that the De Maupassant story did, by God, still fit! The first fifty pages were *good*, and as his notes indicated he could (and did) take the novel from there, setting himself 150 more pages, so the manuscript would total 200, which seemed (and it was) possible, as while having detailed his notes he had been able to block out his chapters. Thus he finished the novel. His agent liked it, so did the publisher, he got the other five thousand — half of which went to paying debts — and the book didn't sell even when remaindered, and as the reviews had been few and not very kind, *The Secret Circle* disappeared into nowhere just as millions of books before it had, and as more millions will, so when his money ran out he went back to his old job. His boss was glad to see him because the corporation had introduced a complicated new product needing nothing less than the best copy to sell. He vowed to his boss he would never write another novel because, he complained, anybody who wants to go through what he did for ten big ones in two payments given at the beginning and end of around three years, has got to be one hundred percent crazy.

***

A year later, on an early summer evening after work in a bar where the copywriters for that company went, a tall, slender, grey-haired man in his mid-fifties approached the man in dark glasses, and asked him if he was who he was, to which the answer yes was given, but as the other, older man, had on introduction an English accent, it turned out he was the English rep for the company, just arrived in the States, and having discovered through conversation that the man in the dark glasses was the one who had written the copy that had made a difficult product easy to sell, the Englishman (on the q.t.), having also read *The Secret Circle*, wanted to meet the author, and, in short, after having chatted a bit, in the social buzz of the cocktail hour, the Englishman startled the author by saying he had enjoyed the book very much, and wanted to know — had the author read Conan Doyle?

"The Holmes stories," responded the man in dark glasses. The author — ex-author.

"Doyle wrote many stories beside the Holmes and even the Professor Challenger stories," explained the Englishman, "and as I in particular enjoyed, and was amused by the ending of your novel, I wondered . . ." he paused to sip his drink — "you see, many years ago, while a student at Cambridge, a group of us decided, for the fun of it, to read

127

all of Doyle, and make a Selected Best Works besides the Holmes and Challenger series, to, we hoped, sell to a publisher, which effort failed, but in two of the books that were my task to read, I read a story called *The Nightmare Room*, and your ending reminded me of that story to a degree so remarkable that I think fit to tell you that you stole it, sir, damned near word for word."

The Englishman smiled.

"Well, yeah," the American admitted. "A couple of years ago I was passing by a second-hand bookstore, and saw a book of stories by Doyle which I bought on a hunch, and that story was in there. I was having a nightmare in my own room trying to finish that Goddamned novel, and when I read the story, well, because of something personal that had happened with a girl in a bar one afternoon, everything clicked."

He paused, then asked —

"Read much De Maupassant?"

"Very little, I'm afraid," the Englishman confessed.

"Good," grinned the man in dark glasses, catching the bartender's eye. "Whatever you're drinking, the next one's on me."

It Is Written on the Wind

—for J. H.

THE SKY WAS PURE and vivid blue, humidity free, and the March sun glared on the city like an optical sledgehammer. Upper halves of skyscrapers glistened blue and silver on glass and steel above a dark, opaque swamp, at the bottom of which foot and auto traffic scurried in shadowed screaming canyon insect glitter. Atlantic winds whipped low down these geometric tunnels, swirling grit and scraps of paper as by giant waving hands — my coat collar up, head down, hands in pockets being spun around walking downtown I thought I saw, but wasn't sure for he was a shadow, but then I was — John, whom I hadn't seen in a dozen dozen moons, I stumbled, fighting the elements in my hurry, shouting —

"John!" I cried. "John!"

Looking peeved, there on the corner, leaning against the wind, waiting for the light to change, but at last he heard me, and turned, saw me, called my name, threw out his arms, in a rush we embraced.

Breathless we spoke, and as chance had it, we both were free that day, so we went to a pleasant sidestreet tap, ordered chilled steins of ale, toasted, drank, and talked. The story is complex, there was much to say, there still is, for within there is another.

* * *

We'd been retail salesmen in the same organization in those days, and both had quit for better jobs, me first, then John. And that was that, didn't hear a word, can't say why, it's a big city, but oh so small, and discreet, when friends and lovers part to go their ways. Yet back a ways I saw our old boss's secretary in Central Park, we greeted each other, and in conversation she said John and his wife were divorced, so, on this windy afternoon in March I mentioned the encounter in the Park, adding that my marriage had also failed — neither marriage had

131

borne children—my ex-wife was happy with another man as she had never been with me, and I can say in fiction that John said the same was true on his side, though that is not the case, although it serves. It was also true (in this sense), that we were at present ourselves happy, each having met a woman we'd never dreamed we would, and things, in short, were swell.

The last I'd seen he'd been too thin, and I won't say too sensitive, but too aware of his duty to his wife, and too resigned, too pale, and day by day too sad, and weary. Yet sitting beside him enjoying the cold ale, how he had changed! Gained weight, looked husky, strong, had good color, prone to rather outrageous laughter, eyes held a fire I'd never seen. His hair—still black—was somewhat shorter, but still long, and combed straight back, but it stood like a brush, and his long sideburns, flanking his high cheekbones, gave his broad and handsome face a rugged midwestern character I'd never—ever seen on him. He's a tall guy, as kind a man as I've ever known. Courteous. A gentleman. Not many men like John. Nay, not many.

We swapped amusing—some very funny—memories about that job. Like me, he has a good memory, and it was—as we agreed—a little disgusting that we remembered even the names of customers—I reminded him of more names, and he did me likewise, reaching a point of intensity where we were having difficulty speaking through laughter, trying to cap the other which we did, until we called a truce, ordered another ale, quarreling over who would pay. Never having felt better he called in sick, took the day off and was out shopping. I was on unemployment—much amusement—I too was out shopping, so Fate had worked Her magic, and in the winds of March, which indeed makes one's heart a dancer, John and I had met.

However, I feel somewhat guilty, for there is that little story saying— *Tell me.*

* * *

For too long in our lives, though neither of us knew it, John and myself had travelled parallel in limbo—his divorce preceded mine, which meant it was after his that he had, one night in the Village, met a woman, dated and gotten serious with her and they became lovers.

Before she went to England on a Fulbright—her exit from John, and for a different reason, my wife's from me. So, as it is and will be, I

132

met a woman at a party midtown — we became lovers, and while out walking one evening we passed the store where John and I had worked, and I mentioned, as one does, that I used to work — I pointed — there.

"John did too!" she exclaimed.

"*John!*"

"Yes, do you know him? I used to go with him."

We laughed — and after I'd told her some job stories involving John, she recalled that once or twice he had mentioned me — "So *you're* the joe! Well, well!" and that night and the next morning — she had an excellent memory — we swapped John's stories — and tied up some loose ends, for example that John, and this for considerable duration, no less, had been first separated from his wife, not yet divorced, which was then, at that present, my state too and I felt a bright green thread go out to John, although I admit I had slight pangs when she said on her return to the States her first thought was to phone him, which she did, and was sorry to hear he was with someone else (it didn't last). She was quick to spot my reaction, told me not to worry, as in all truth she was curious about John and wanted to see how he was doing, because he had been in considerable distress because of his separation, she had worked hard mending him, she said, and when she had gone overseas, she had felt guilt in leaving him in his still painful state. It had nothing to do with any overt, or too-condescending intentions on her part — she had been drawn to him — but she did have expectations, and as she was an empathetic person, she wondered if she had failed him. He had wanted to respond, and although things looked good on the surface, she was aware that the more they were together, the worse it got, and on her return from England she felt justified in wanting to know how he was. I agreed, saying I too had wondered, but hadn't phoned him because of my own problems, which I felt I had to solve alone before I became hypocritical and started solving the problems of others.

She asked if I had seen him, I said no, but, I added, there will be a day. She asked, if I did see him would I write her and let her know how he was? I said of course, and not long after she went to California, where she is still teaching. Or so I heard. Our relationship was, in fact, brief, and because she was doing some last minute research, working with a professor at Columbia, we didn't see each other, as I think of it, but two or three nights a week, so we were lovers of sorts, which meant we were friends, and when she left the farewell was warm, which meant that I didn't know her very well, although I knew her . . . a little, because you see, when she spoke of John as she had, I did, in that way, get to know her — through John, for I was in John's shoes, and as John and I had worked side by side for so long I knew him, in his shoes listening to her, I wondered what John had thought — and felt. I knew what I thought, as well as what I was feeling, and if my judgement of John was any good at all, I was pretty sure I knew what was going on, for if anything had happened to him like what was happening to me, with her, why was she lying? and this is what I was thinking as I sat beside him that March afternoon, drinking ale in a sidestreet saloon, not knowing how to ask him, or if I should, because it was so clear he was happy — wasn't I? — yet —

Why had she lied?

"There is something on your mind," he smiled. "I've seen that look before."

"Why," I asked, side-stepping, "were you so vexed on the corner?"

"Macy's was out of the sweaters I wanted, and I was on my way to Alexander's, which is not what is on your mind."

I put my hand on his shoulder.

"Remember Blondie?"

He paled, and was for a moment speechless, but then asked — had I known her?

I nodded.

I said, "Skip that part. I want to know why she lied to me."

"Lie?" he frowned. "Her? She was as honest as anyone I've ever met. She never lied to me — what did she say? What was it about?"

"You."

*   *   *

Her astonishing intellect, sense of individual identity, dazzling humor and blonde, California beach-bunny image — her intellect was knocked out by her nickname: she could have been in the movies.

And what a real person. Affectionate, kind, faithful, fun to be with, willing to do things, sharp and bright at home and in company, eager for other points of view, pragmatic, funny, almost diabolical in scholarship, talked back in Latin at televised Spanish quiz shows — too spontaneous in her attitude and too sensitive to manipulate it, she was dedicated to her work, loved people, loved to teach, enjoyed being home, and the outdoor life too, museums, concerts, hiking, camping, vivid, self-assured. She had a great future.

134

And in all honesty, she wasn't the liar. I am. What I said to John was in part true, because the whole truth wasn't to the point, that afternoon. It was so good to see you again, my old friend . . . I last saw Blondie in San Francisco, and my departure was . . .

* * *

As John talked about her, it came clear that her certain language with me about him was in part necessary. Not because the truth was beyond her, but in her complicated (or, who knows? maybe simple) emotional structure, there were things she wouldn't admit, and as I listened, everything John said tallied. His story matched mine.

Who wanted to give her up? What man could, or would? She cast a spell, and as living with a futuristic creature from Antiquity he was spellbound, and in suspense, so when he came home from work and she ceased her studies, and embraced him anew, in a tailwind blast that took him away, so no matter what he knew, by heart, by full experience, nothing had happened, they had just met, it was their first night, and as she kissed him and snuggled next to him, reality was lighting a straight fuse to explosion.

Well, he said, somewhat hurt by my having told him what she had said, they had in fact broken up before she went to England. He had lost a good deal of weight, and in a gathering depression, at having to come home to her every day, he realized he was as haunted as he looked, which at last he confessed to her.

"I'm worn out."

"I suspected it." Pause, voice soft — "I can't help it. You know."

"Yes. Have the others said the same?"

She nodded. "Most. Some sooner than you. Some later. Some like it." Sleepy-eyed smile: "Them, I can do without."

"Why?"

"It's the way I am."

"There's a reason."

"I love it, I want it, I get it because I do it — my way. It — has to be." Pause. With a sigh. "Okay, I'll go."

Packing clothes, a box of books, crossed the room to him, put her hands on his cheeks, body close to his, gazed up in his eyes, parted her lips —

"I'd rather stay. I like you, I hoped it wouldn't be so soon, John. John.

135

I've given you everything, and taken more." She smiled, blue eyes hard, as she whispered, "Is something missing?"

"No. You're all here," he said. "And that's the trouble."

"Why?" lowering her voice—"am I not enough?—I mean, as a friend, and—"

"I'm lost," he frowned, and they embraced—she embraced him, rather, as he stood and gazed over her head, his arms at his sides. The word he wanted was tender.

"I want you to leave," he said. "Come. I'll catch you a cab."

Her plane was leaving in a few days. Four—five? He couldn't remember.

"Can't I—at least stay tonight?" she asked, surprised.

"No. I want you to go."

She gave him a long look, and finished packing. There wasn't much, but—as always—there was enough. She put on her camel's hair coat, and blue silk scarf, looking at him. There was nothing hidden in her look, in fact it had a certain transparency, and way back there, he saw something he couldn't comprehend.

"All right," she smiled. "I understand."

"You like to spend last nights with—us, don't you?"

"I prefer it. It's my way."

"To prefer?"

"Well, it's my last chance to—to be with—you. As it was with—others, yes. I love being with men. If you were asked to leave, wouldn't you want to spend the last night?" Pause. "With me?"

"No."

Her voice was kind, and unreal. "Perhaps I'm different. Will you kiss me?"

"No. Let's go."

"Go? you say. Where shall I go?"

"You've got money, and there are hotels. Make a reservation."

She crossed to the telephone table, and as she bent to take out the phone book he said,

"Phone from the lobby."

She straightened, turned to him, frowned, bit her lip. As hurt as she was surprised, the combination made her more beautiful, vulnerable and tender-seeming than he had ever seen her. Or known her. And in the illusion his body began to flame, although, good God he knew better, in a quick move, picked up her two suitcases, she picked up the small box of papers and books, as well as her briefcase, they went to the door, out, into an elevator, next they were in the lobby, and she had made a hotel reservation.

The doorman caught the cab, and John helped him with her luggage. The cabby got in behind the wheel, John opened the rear door, and Blondie stood, looking at him, a little at a loss for words.

"Will you write?" she asked.

"No," he said.

They shook hands, she got in the cab, he closed the door, she rolled down the window, he said,

"Goodbye. Take care of yourself."

Turned, walked back into his apartment house, through the lobby to the elevator, back up and into his apartment, as Blondie's cab drove to her hotel.

Because of the scent of her perfume, her body, and the residue of her very self, he opened the windows, stripped the bed, and began the lengthy process of clearing away every trace. Clear in his purpose but moved puppet-like, as if a voice was directing him, thus he obeyed, and after—a week or so, one evening coming home from work, his apartment smelled fresh, or—it smelled as it seemed, like his and him. Of his soap, his aftershave lotion, his shampoo, and as he was a neat person, of the brand name furniture and floor polish he used. He sat down in his—his—armchair, with a can of Bud and watched the evening news. And following that, went to the closet, and way back on the top shelf, where they were hidden, he slid boxes forward, selecting a jigsaw puzzle that had bothered him, almost all white, and stark dark blue, covered bridge in winter, *Moonlight in Vermont*, set up his card table, she'd been inept—as she admitted—with jigsaw puzzles, beside herself in laughter, and tonight he was glad. Felt non-aesthetic, a trifle anonymous. Liked that best of all. Stretched his legs, inhaled, rubbed his hands together, smiled, leaned forward, removed the lid, emptied the box on the table, and after putting the box on the rug, turned all the pieces face up, and began on the edges.

Realized he was hungry. Went into his kitchenette, and made supper, which included a small salad, the kind he had enjoyed at home, in Minnesota, as a boy, involving potatoes in none but that one way. Sat at the small, formica-topped table and ate, no question about it, someone was missing, and it would be a while before she'd be gone in a complete way, but he had made a beginning, and, in all truth, "she was gone," and that was final.

He never saw her again, but if through any cause he was reminded—in that endless pattern of associations—she occurred to him, he isolated the association, considered it, and decided

"A page is missing!"   Turn this one.

why she had chosen me, but I saw she was frightened, couldn't speak, rattled and sad in the bright sun, a brilliant, beautiful young woman saying goodbye to a man who had found the secret she had given him — a sudden sizzling bluewhite bolt sears the darkness beyond my desk, thunder rocks this midnight room, silver rainstreaks slash my windows, cascading onto the dark, deserted street below, ah, it is of place and circumstance — written on the wind, John, your way I had chosen to say farewell, was she beginning to see? perhaps hoping — but she didn't know how, nor would ever dare to ask, nay, John, she would not be told by me, it was her way, *not mine to tell her, but her will to change, and for whom? Me? You? Why?* Tears sparkled in her eyes, we shook hands, I walked through the boarding tunnel onto the big ship and flew away. At 37,000 feet, in blue skies I gazed down through clouds at the ocean, bay, and the city curled in a Macedonian field of view, under a low pale yellow ochre blanket of smog. I had a drink and a smoke. Never saw her again.

"Sure?"

No.

In Flanders' Fields

—for Elsene

HE WAS STANDING at the bar in the restaurant, talking with Mr. Richardson, the bartender—a rather courting kind of man whom I disliked. I joined them, and after saying hello and farewell to Mr. Richardson, we sat at a table and ordered drinks telling the waitress it'd be a few minutes before we'd want to see menus.

I could see by his face that he was tired and angry but most of all perplexed. I was tired too, but not angry or perplexed, so I asked him how his job had gone. He said the usual, to which I agreed about my job. Then I asked him what was wrong.

He's a good-looking man in his early forties with clear black and brown eyes, arched eyebrows, a straight slender nose, thin lips and dimples with a feminine quality I find becoming. He's a little over six feet tall, he's slender, and were it not for the fact that his face shows his emotions, he would look like most men, but as he is in general feeling something, his face becomes unique, as does his body, for his body changes too. When uncertain his features tighten, and his body becomes as if wary of itself. His lips part, and from under a concentrated scowl his eyes fix on a distant target, he thinks hard then, for he is angry, and he thinks fast, for he wants to solve the matter. It is perhaps that I am a sentimental woman, or perhaps that I love him that I see how striking he is when angry, and how his body fixes into itself, and the whole man becomes complete, and alert, in direct but complementary opposition to his agile, sleek, even silky warm and happy self, or both combined in his passion. Yet I don't think he's an exceptional man, except in my eyes of course, for I've known exceptional men, and in most cases they are easy enough to live with but too one-sided, because their being exceptional creates their precise limitations, for they live within themselves. To live with genius is impossible, because genius is the final limit, style, and sacrifice. Which, as far as the sexes go, applies to exceptional women, as well as to women of genius, from a man's point of view, yet from a woman's point of view not quite the same, because she is more complicated than he.

I don't consider myself exceptional although he does. The years we've been together have been good, considering my vindicative quality (which angers him), and, because vindication, with vengence kin, confuses him, he gets more angry because what angers him to the verge of loss of control, is confusion. I suspect his vulnerability to confusion, and his true anger, goes way back. I know very little about textbook psychology, but I'm no fool, experience has taught me much, and he has spoken of his parents in such a way that I see his early confusion. Not that he blows up, starts screaming and throwing his fists or the china, no, but his fight to clear himself from confusion is a deep and violent one, which removes him from me, causing me to be introspective too, and if I am the cause, I become guilty, and angry at myself, and just like him, try to work my way out, while he has that look of his, and won't talk until he's arrived at a point that satisfies him. In the two years before his wife divorced him, as well as the year after, he was in therapy, and since then, if in a jam he can't comprehend or rationalize, he gets in touch with his doctor. I'm a coward in that respect. My vindictiveness frightens me. I lose control, and to be honest become a person I dislike to a degree that unnerves me, and I admit I don't want to know why. Our few fights have centered around this issue. He doesn't walk out on me, and go to the bar like my ex-husband did. This man I love stays, and fights me. I like, even love that, because I can count on him, his conviction and determination blended in with his anger and love form a rare jewel indeed, and because both of us are so sensitive to each other, we have, if I may say so, a remarkable relationship. In terms of little things, he isn't — nor am I — neurotic about order. As long as what we want is within reach and not under a pile of dirty socks and underwear, we're happy. The studio we live in is kept in the kind of mess that between us a half hour's work cleans up.

* * *

We are not married. He was for ten years. I was for seven. My husband and our two daughters were killed in an automobile accident five years ago, two years before I met the man sitting across from me (angry, perplexed), sipping a straight up gin martini with an olive, two of which he enjoys before supper. Two. That's all. A glass or two of cold beer with lunch. My husband had been drunk and misjudged a turn. It was

142

all much more than a nightmare, following the usual grim formalities which many of us know. The call from the police. The visit to the morgue, and, in short, the beginning of a new life. The suburbs were a dead end to me, and so was my country, so I sold the house for less than it was worth, and because my husband had investments and savings that through his will came to me—I didn't know he had made a will, which meant he had had a foreknowledge of death, and, so his lawyers told me, left everything to me. I cashed in his investments and savings, and with the money from the sale of the house I went to Europe. I had studied French in college, and could read and write a little as well as speak that language, and though I never was an outgoing person, with money and language as my tools, I considered myself lucky for I had much more than most women in my circumstance, and being a good-looking, however anxious and compulsive widow, I was at the age for change, and with Paris as my base of operations, I travelled far and wide, slept with many men in many countries, lived an exciting, desperate life, became involved with all forms of drugs, exotic and otherwise, with opium as my favorite, and, in general, as Moll might put it, I whored around Europe for a year and a half. I bought beautiful clothes, learned to be a modern and continental woman, so I could ask pretty high prices for whatever pleasures the men wanted, which was often everything, but as my expenses were heavy, and I worked hard at keeping my body trim, I always seemed to need more money, so as part of my effort I turned to X-rated films, in a few of which I starred, being, as they said, very good, and having saturated myself with culture, I was, they said, fine company, so I was given access to opportunities of stealing that were rare and, for I was bold, I took advantage, which brought me into a different circle of the underworld, and though, because I was a respectable whore, in dealing jewels and furs, etc., as well as drugs, I found my two occupations overlapped, and I had to perform double duties often whether I liked it or not, so as I burnt a path across Europe I became less reputable, the payoffs were heavy, and using disguises and faked passports I became a hunted woman, and as such, was caught in what thieves call an innocent act, i.e., looking at something I was going to steal but had not yet stolen, but when I was booked, and because of the computer system my identity was discovered and I was put in prison in a country I won't mention, but had it not been for a businessman I'd met in Venice, I might still be in that prison, a place of horror to this day, unchanged since Defoe gave his universal description.

I don't know how the businessman—who said he was American—

143

did it, but he did. I never asked him how—I don't ask anyone that, unless they want to tell me, and this being my circumstance then, I learned again as I had so often before, that there are two sides of police corruption. I also don't know how to justify his doing it for me. Our original meeting was casual, we talked over coffee, he gave me his business card saying if he could help me to let him know. I didn't quite know what to say, but several weeks later I saw him sitting alone in a restaurant in London, I joined him and it was as if an old friend—I suspect I reminded him of someone, for he wanted only my company, and it was strange, for I saw him again, not long after, in Rome, then in Berlin, and later in Nice. We developed an affection for each other, and upon my clandestine release from prison, we drove in his car to Spain, and thence to Portugal by plane, and as I had no clothes but what I was wearing, nor any cash—my lawyer, a thief, had seen to that—the American set me up in a room of my own in a small hotel near a beach in Portugal, and because the weather was warm my necessities for dress were simple, and as I had grown more than weary of that new life I'd discovered, which had aged me so, I wanted more than I could say to be left alone, which he understood. He never made an advance of any kind, not one touch except in friendship—not that I wouldn't have let him, for sure I would have. Hadn't I hundreds of others? Yet I discovered, no—no, I didn't want that and it seems to me amazing that he didn't either. His eyes, when our glances met, gazed upon me as upon someone loved and lost. . .

He left on business the next day, and a pattern began. He visited me every two weeks, stayed two days and then left again, to again return. I'll admit at first I distrusted his generosity—who, who would believe it? Wasn't there always a catch—somewhere?

But in any event, I began to get myself in shape. I swam and lay on sand in the sun, my short hair grew long, I lost my pallor and so too the hard, uncaring eyes of the whore and the thief. My body became full, round, tan, and with my long dark hair, I caught many an eye wherever I or we went, and in the simple beauty of casual beachwear, plus a little stolen jewelry I'd managed to keep, we made a handsome couple indeed. He looked somewhat like Jean Gabin.

I should confess that this account is not—so far—true in the way I want, because I felt guilty because I had, by omission, or silence, kept something from him, while he was being so kind. I had kept a dozen or so fine jewels, and having vowed to never again be what I had been, my deepest possessive self forbade mention of them to anyone.

Thus, as the weeks turned into months, the lives I had led fell behind

144

me. Through borrowing books from tourists and while knowing French and learning Spanish, I read books of all sorts in three languages, and in so doing, became conscious, introspective, and prone to long walks alone. I began to like myself. I enjoyed my own company! and began to cherish being alone, which my angel businessman also began to realize, ah such a kind man, and it was in this sense, on our walks, or at meals together, our conversations changed, and I began to talk about job possibilities back in the States. What did he think? He got a warm, candlelit look in his eyes saying he'd see to it, which he did, and to be brief, as I was broke he gave me money and a one-way ticket to JFK, with two letters of introduction to advertising firms in New York.

I was traveling light, so baggage was no problem, and while saying farewell to my Angel I had tears of gratitude in my eyes, my heart soft and yet strong. We embraced, kissed, and I went through customs as a breeze through trees, in a smart new blue dress, my hair piled high on my head — concealing the jewels I'd saved, as there was a chance they were still hot enough to be on lists at American customs. The money he had given me was generous enough (I vowed to pay him back and I kept that vow), to get me an apartment, although the down payment would leave me thirty days to get the next month's rent, so if I didn't get a job fast I would be in danger for sure. Imagine a woman my age in that city, alone with no place to live. It was beneath my new pride and determination to go a-begging to my dead husband's friends or family, or business acquaintances, all of whom I'd never liked anyway, nor they me, so if worst came to worst, through criminal contacts I'd made overseas I knew a name or two in New York, before whom I could let my hair down. But in that necessity I made another vow — no matter what, that would be my last contact with the underworld anywhere, I burned that vow into my heart, because the last words my Saviour had said, holding my face in his hands, and his eyes on mine, shining with kindness and strength —

"In your life ahead of you, remember, my darling, in the eye of God, all that was, will yet be new."

I wept in grace.

Those words cancelled the police call, cancelled the death of my children, and my husband. And all I had done in Europe. In my rejuvenated life I saw then, at the airport, that death and spiritual disfiguration had been the catalyst, and my Angel the support for the agent of change to take full control, so with my life before me and my fate as my fact, I would follow, and that I did.

My mind was as clear as the TWA sky. My spirit as green and fierce as the Atlantic below.

At JFK the landing was smooth.

I rented a hotel room, then found a furnished apartment not as expensive as I had expected, and then days later, after having failed at the first ad agency, I was taken on as Girl Friday in the second, took an advance on my salary and bought some clothes, and my life began. I mastered the art of layout, learned how to talk telephone diplomacy, and because I had developed an excellent memory from stealing, it wasn't long before I had the job down pat, and a few months later was assistant to production, and a few months afterwards was an account executive, and having, through quick wits, caught a couple of new clients on my own — on the telephone!, I received a handsome commission, so at the end of a year and a half I was making a pretty good salary. I moved into a better apartment in a good neighborhood, furnished it myself and, in short, having done far more than I ever dreamed, I was a successful, popular and envied person in a very new world.

From the beginning, however, each week I set aside a small sum, which, with my salary increasing, also increased, and at year's end I mailed my Angel the money I owed, to his address in London. I wrote him a nice letter (we'd kept in touch with postcards), and I enclosed a glossy photo of me at my job, looking very handsome and Woman On The Way Up standing next to my boss going over layouts, as he listened, face serious. But the letter I wrote, thanking my Samaritan was not an easy one to write, I can tell you, for in certain matters of the heart, words must be few, and in truth rather plain.

Therefore, I should mention that I have, in a hidden compartment in the bottom of a shoddy sewing kit my mother gave me, a small, dark blue satin cloth which is folded around my jewels, because — just as before — no matter what comes, including the deepest love, a woman has to take care of a different form of love, which is of her life itself, meaning, in a word, survival.

I became, as I've said, popular. Many men took me out, and many men made many promises, a few seeming true, as well as reasonable, but through it all I maintained a control, with one exception. He was a good, kind and generous man, yet I had met the best man of all, my Angel, so warmth, generosity, understanding, kindness and — patience, were known to me in the same way whores and thieves knew caution, suspicion, distrust, and danger. But although those days were over, their residue remained in my eyes in the form of sophistication, which made me something of a mystery, and in their male eyes I saw the question — *Who is she? What has she done? What is that look?* I answered in secret: *"Never tell!"*

146

The man who was the exception, a kind and generous man, I met by chance at a bar while with my boss. We fell into conversation, and in short, after several dates beginning in the spring and lasting to the late fall, which involved expensive restaurants, box seats in Yankee Stadium, first run movies, gallery and museum openings as well as small parties with his friends, it became a little difficult to say goodnight — get out of the cab, and after entering my apartment house, and taking the elevator up and going to bed — I knew he was hurt, and puzzled. He had had a bad divorce a couple of years before, and was paying alimony. He didn't expect anything of me, he believed (as did I) that Nature would take Her course, a most difficult set of arrangements was coming into view that put me on the sway. We had attended the first night production of a new musical and the party afterwards, but didn't stay long, or, stayed long enough to have a little too much champagne, and then went to a small Italian restaurant, had a fine late supper with smooth wine and I knew what was coming.

He flagged down the cab — he didn't like to drive his own car in the city — and we drove around the park, and then to my address. The cab stopped, my friend told the cabby to keep the meter running which was kind of him, for it gave me an escape, while placing the responsibility of the decision on me, which wasn't so kind, but I was beginning to yield, and he knew the decision was mine.

"Tell me," he asked. "What's with you? I see something in your face, or — in you that I can't figure out. You're damned good-looking, but you're not beautiful, you're not out of *Vogue* or Hollywood, so tell me the mystery. Why are your eyes veiled?"

Our arms were linked, our voices soft.

He had told me he despised gossip, and as sad stories made him angry because he was helpless to act, he had told me tales of lives ruined, and how hurt he had been. He was a rare man for sure. Bright, amusing, sensitive, yet tough, and could keep cool. I knew he'd be silent.

I sighed, and bit my lip, for I was guilty, and feeling a hypocrite, but in my inner ear I heard my Angel. I said —

"There is no mystery. It is as it was, I am what I am, no more and perhaps much less."

"That's evasive."

"If it is then I am. In reality I'm not. There are things I won't say, not because I can't, but because in truth — to myself, I forbid it."

"That's better," he smiled. "We're getting warmer."

I turned to face him, and in the darkness, for which I was glad, he couldn't see how pale I had become.

147

"All right," I said. "You touched me there, because — I must tell you — only one has before you, and my decision has been that there will be no getting close to me. I don't know why. In a way I do. It seems either simple or very complicated, but in a true way I don't know the cause. I feel something isn't yet complete, and something within me forbids me to be close with any one but myself. So, what you see in my face, or in my eyes, the veil, might be what the *forbidden* is made of — so real it shows. I hadn't known that. I see questions in men's eyes, but not in yours, for you see me, but — which causes me guilt, as I feel the hypocrite, because you've been so good to me, yet you will never see beyond that veil."

"You know how to hurt."

"Honesty can be painful. You know I don't want to hurt — I know that perhaps you, in a way you love me, and we should in our natures be lovers, as I like you, I trust you, and I believe you."

"Will any man see through the veil?"

"I can't say. How can I? But in a truth chilly enough — I don't care. I can't care."

I shouldn't have said I can't. He had an opening, but he missed it.

"How can you live?" he asked. "How can you be and not know? You're not a cold fish, a castrator or latent beyond touch. What I can't understand is you are — at center — a good-looking, normal, smart, sharp but not brilliant or exceptional woman with your passion held at bay, and I'm crazy about you."

"I like that," I smiled. "Thank you. I never considered myself exceptional or beautiful. I like myself, and when I'm alone, although this may shock you, I love myself. My body is at peace, not at war as so many millions of bodies — it isn't a matter of sex, but a matter of spirit, my own spirit, and so that I may survive in my love, I create barriers to protect me."

"Not many women could say that."

"Few women dare to."

"Peace of body," he murmured, "and love of self. These are new to me. I know peace of mind, and love of an ideal, but not of myself."

"If you can't love yourself, how can you love anyone else?"

"That's your secret, then, isn't it," he said, not asking.

"It would be your secret too, if you did."

"Well, you sure put my Goddamned ego in place."

"I like your ego," I said. "It seems to be in place, but love is different from ego. Love is as natural as snowfall. But the ego knows what it wants, and goes out and gets it. Snow gets nothing, except to touch." Pause.

"And melt," I added.

"My ex-wife hated my ego."

"She hates hers, then."

He was silent. And I opened the door, got out, and as I closed the door —

"She hated herself as well as her ego," he said, sliding across the seat and looking up at me. "Wait," he said, rolling down the window, putting his right elbow on the sill, his left on the back of the front seat. "I won't ask you how you've come to that love, that's your business, not mine, but I realize what you said a moment ago, that you can't care, is a revealing statement, and no doubt one I should pursue, but let me put it this way. You being what you are, however you came to be so, are still in process, and part of your secret is to guard that process to its completion and your fulfillment, which lets me out. Okay," he nodded, "I don't like it, maybe I'm jealous, but — I'm not going to say goodbye to you, and for God's sake let's not be friends. I will say thank you. I do envy you, and, if you can believe it, me being with you at a sudden loss of words. Well, thank you for that too. I'll be thinking about you, and about me, but in all truth more about me than thee."

We smiled.

"If I come up with something, can we get together?"

"You know where I work."

"I do indeed. One last question. Will you be honest with me?"

"I promise."

And through the open window, kissed my hand, smiled goodnight, and as I smiled in return and walked toward the glass doors of my apartment building, I looked back to see the cab pull away, as the doorman held the door for me.

One can imagine how I felt. Sleep was difficult that night. Honest men are hard to find these days, and the fact that he would begin an intropsective process through me and what I had said, was fantastic, and that he had grasped my words without a trace of manipulation, was remarkable, and his saying he would think more about himself than me — while not even seeing me!, was, I felt, the voice of his individuality, and personal spirit. Wasn't that a turn of the tables? Didn't they always say — I'll be thinking of you?

Who was I to deny him? And how right he had been! Good-looking but not beautiful. Not brilliant, and not exceptional. Normal, with passion held at bay, yet there he was off, yet he was correct because I was

149

still in process. Passion! My body! Oh my passion was there, not held at bay, but at peace in itself, dormant, blood flowing warm — my wonderful body! and I beheld myself in the mirror, and in my heart, too, enjoying my peace, and trusting it, as I undressed, showered off all makeup, and after applying a cream to my face and body, I slid between my sheets, naked and warm. I knew how rare it was! I knew! He didn't!

Thus I slept.

Several days later I was obliged to go to an evening party. We had worked all day at the office, and then through supper until nine. We had a new client whom we were anxious to keep. The money would be considerable, and would get us into a new location, and out of our present cramped quarters, so when my boss and I took the cab we were still talking shop, and not long after, walking into the apartment we were talking more shop, but on being handed drinks — we looked at each other, grinned, touched glass rims and winked.

"For God's sake!" he cried.

"No more shoptalk!" I laughed, turned, and was introduced by one of our salesmen, to the host of the party, a tall greying man with fake warm eyes who had gotten a foundation grant for research into an area, he smiled, so far neglected, and —. I saw a hustler.

But the drink was delicious, and gesturing to my boss I crossed the crowded room, sat on a long sofa, lit a cigarette — I smoke on rare occasions and that day had been one — leaned back, exhaled, and stared into space as a body sat next to me, and thinking it was my boss, I turned. It wasn't. It was a man in his late thirties, wearing a blue and white seersucker jacket, blue buttondown shirt, faded jeans, sweatsocks and natural colored moccasins. He was angry. He said —

"Sorry I sat down so hard."

"I didn't notice," I said. "I'm pretty spacey — at work all day."

"What do you do?"

I answered him, and we talked in that way until it seemed to arrive at what he wanted to say from the beginning.

"I hate these parties, and am asking myself my Usual Question: What am I doing here?"

"Weren't you invited?"

"Yes. He always invites me."

"I don't understand," I said.

"This guy is a grant hustler," said the stranger. "I've known him for years. You've heard of grant hustlers?"

150

"There's a lot of variations on the hustle," I said. "Don't you approve of grants?"

"No, I like to work for my money."

"I see," I said. "That's a switch."

He looked at me, and looked again, I guess, and I was a little unsettled. His eyes, as his face, changed, seemed to find a focus, yet he was not apart from himself, and his gaze was steady.

"Tell me more about your job," he said, with a slight smile. "Or, better said — and which I shouldn't ask — what have you done in your life? Where have you been? You look like you've seen Hell itself."

"We've been working since eight this morning, that's eleven straight hours, and anybody who—"

"I don't mean that," he interrupted (I was willing to be interrupted), "what's that I see in your eyes? Well, I like it! Hardboiled experience, pain, greed, pleasure, got some secrets? I do. *The Lady from Shanghai* is at the Carnegie Cinema, want to go? She's fantastic."

"She?"

"Rita Hayworth. She and Welles were married then, he cut her hair, dyed it blonde, starred in it with her and directed it."

I cleared my throat and put out my cigarette, not quite knowing, again, what to say.

"It's a marvelous movie."

Say yes. Say yes!

I don't know why — God knows I've handled some fast hitters before, but I said — yes, yes, I'll go! — comic breathless.

We agreed to meet in the theatre lobby the next evening, at an appointed hour, and then we talked. He was the assistant manager of a mail order firm, and enjoyed making wood sculptures at home, although, he admitted, they weren't any good, but he enjoyed making them anyway. He also liked his job.

"Do you drink much?" I asked.

"An interesting question, up front like you put it, therefore I see it matters. No, I don't drink much. I used to, not a lot, though, but much more than I — two martinis before supper are my limit. I like a glass or two of beer with lunch."

"Why don't you drink? You seem the nervous type" — I made a shaky smile — "or are you in complete control?"

"No, and not to shock you, but I like myself too much. I'm happy except when I'm confused. Drunks enjoy confusion, but I like, even love being happy, and therefore like, even love myself. Sorry about that."

I parted my lips to speak, but because I felt something snap, and yield in me, I fell silent, at a loss for words, looking into my drink, which I finished and put on the end table beside me, and turned to face him on the sofa, and looking square into those most honest brown eyes, I said:

"I don't drink much either, and almost never smoke. I like myself, I even—I too love myself. My husband was a drunkard, and in an auto accident well over three years ago was killed along with our two daughters. I sold our suburban house, and with the savings and investments he had left me, I went to Europe, and—." I told him the tale. He smiled.

"Not bad. I know you. My saviour was a cop who said if he caught me again it was prison without fail. This was in a small city in the north west, we got to know each other, a little. Then I left town, wandered around the country, thinking and thinking, going from job to job until I found this one, and worked my way up, to where I am—it's great to meet you."

He told me his name, and I told him mine.

"There's more I'll tell you," he said, "which includes opium—my favorite, but, as you know, the details are tawdry." He paused. "And thank God those days and the dreadful nights are behind me."

I agreed. I went to the movie with him the next night. We both loved it, and afterwards I spent the night with him, in his studio loft downtown, witnessing my body open outward in his embrace, and yet curve and curl in, to please itself, and make me happy.

***

In the next year and then two years our close as well as casual conversation brought out the details of our lives, although, as I didn't tell him everything, nor did he tell me, there were a few things beyond question.

With our combined salaries we got a large, very open loft near the river, so he could have plenty of space to sculpt (he was right, they weren't very good), and as I had in a sense discovered books in that hotel in Portugal I began to build an impressive library, starting with the classics, and as the sun and moon rolled around I sectioned out my reading. I began with the English novel, went to the French, Russian, Spanish, German and Italian novels, and because poets and philosophers were quoted, I began to read them too, all of which, I realized, would take me the rest of my life, but in the fascinating cross-references novelists make, I discovered a new kind of world and began reading biography, autobiography, and history, my mind opened out and I began taking notes on the references, which led a writer friend to write a paper, using my discovery in Fielding, which was, to my pleasure, accepted by an English literary review. The paper was in fact dedicated to me, although I admit, seeing my name in print gave me a little jolt, for sure.

Well, our lives went on. He went to his job in the morning and I to mine. We did nothing sensational, led rather ordinary stay-at-home lives which to some no doubt seemed dull. But he liked his job, I liked mine, and every once in a while, not too often, but not too seldom either, we seized the happy opportunity to make what we called a long night, and they were wonderful, with our bodies, chilled wine, and opium.

* * *

"What's wrong?" I asked.

"I don't know what to think. The damnedest thing happened today, and I can't figure it out."

"Making you angry, as always."

"Yes, but which I'll not be when I solve it."

"May I help?" I asked, sipping my drink. "Not knowing why you're puzzled, if you'd tell me, maybe—"

"Well," he sighed, rubbing his chin. "Discretion, discretion, what to do?"

"Perhaps I can tell you. Being a former whore, thief and general all-around bad girl running parallel with you, I feel I can confess something that might relate to your discretion. Want to hear?"

He looked at me—a reproachful look—but with a smile, and said—

"That woman's intuition stuff is original common sense. But call it any name, it's important. Men swaggering or tip-toeing around town don't, they think, need it. They do, but they won't admit it. So, me knowing you as I do, I have a hunch you're thinking it involves another woman, so in spite of my confusion and the follow-up anger I feel, I'm telling you that I don't want you to go into one of your vicious—"

"I won't. I promise."

"What I don't like about you is that you remember these things, and

153

use them against me."

"Look," I said, "I'm working on that. You know it and you should hear my story before you—. It's natural I think what I do because as I know you, and you mutter something about discretion, my common sense, not my intuition, tells me a woman is involved. True?"

"True."

"All right. I've felt a little unhappy myself. There's something I haven't told you. I've wanted to, but felt it had to come full circle, to complete itself, before I could."

I paused, thinking, before I said—

"In the strict sense, nothing happened. But it all but did, which means, therefore, something did happen."

His eyes were on me, and our eyes met. I like that. One two three. Yes, I love it.

A form appeared between our faces, hovering there, connecting and holding us in suspense, beyond our ken as the space between sea and sky, silent and invisible, but in its slow whirl and spin it gave out a low inaudible hum, a solar wind which seemed to speak a conjecture in the style of a riddle *suppose*, it began, while seeming to continue, that the hills and the trees, clouds and all water anywhere and all earth everywhere, as the stars on the Other Side below out feet are in the Eye suggesting the form of a speaking brain with continental sections, jungles, forests, wild life or tame in all forms cells and the rivers, lakes and seas fluid brain alive *suppose* that brain, seeming the most tiny particle within the universe of an atom might be the brain of our universe, fixed out—from the Milky Way in a sprawling galactic body—would we say we know where we are? and what we are? savage spatial microbes on a spinning brain? and the so-called past but a form of organic revenge, the future a form of anyway, and the present the shape of a well-fed cat?

Not knowing where in a non-existent when, windblown and growing, silent and invisible an unseen line loops out into space for its inevitable contact, and she answers his question in a supposition of truth:

"When did he call?"

Four months ago, she replied, admitting she had lied saying she had to work late, but the lie was preferred to the rather complicated and incomplete truth because it gave her freedom of action.

She agreed to meet him in his apartment. She had been there before, only twice, because she didn't like the spoor his ex-wife had left, although she had been relaxed, and felt safe. There wasn't any reason to feel otherwise.

154

But as she rang the doorbell of his apartment, and stood in the hallway, she felt alien, and when he opened the door he was different. Her first impulse, out of her regard for him, was to check her alien feeling and her own eyes seeing he was different, but as she made that denial she denied it, because one step into his apartment and she knew she was right. He was different, something was wrong, she felt cautious, and threatened.

He offered her a glass of wine which she accepted, and as they talked he made himself a Scotch and soda, they sat on the sofa before the fireplace, pleasant fire burning, and continued talking. But — she asked him, what was wrong? Why was his face crooked? Was he ill? He made a little snicker by way of reply, and said maybe he was ill, but he'd done a lot of thinking, and still couldn't figure her out, and with a gathering frustration and anger he said he realized he had to know what her secret was. What was that mystery that baffled him so! She began to get angry, but controlled herself saying there was no secret and she couldn't understand, after over a year and a half, why he was going on like this. He said he had to know. She said he couldn't know everything. He said he could know as much as he could stand. She said she didn't get it. He said what he meant was he had to find out enough to satisfy him. She asked why he had said as much as he could stand? beginning to be frightened — cities in Europe, flashing her their signals! She asked how much he had found out. He said a lot. She said you mean as much as you can stand — more. He said yes. She asked him why he wasn't ashamed of himself. He said he was but that didn't count. She asked why. He said she knew. She said she guessed she did know, but if he knew as much as he wanted, why did he want to fuck her? Didn't what he had found out disgust him? He said no, he liked it. She said what he meant was he wanted to rape her and he said yes and there was nothing she could do about it. She asked him what that meant. He said he had a dossier plus prints of the porno films. She asked if he had watched them. He said yes. So it's blackmail, she said. He again said yes, but she was a faster thinker than he was and she said let me think. Think all you want, he said, not realizing she had arrived at her plan. I'm through thinking, she said. He said, What? You heard me, she said. It didn't take much work, did it? No, he said. You used your real name at first. My married name, she said, on the legal documents, medical papers, passport, etc. He said yes. She said the rest was easy. Yes, he said. She looked at him.

She was humming.

She said if he thought that the final secret of her mystery would be found in her body he was mistaken. He had the wrong body. He said he didn't care, he knew what he wanted and he wanted her body, right or wrong. She said he was a coward, he agreed, she said he was a liar, he agreed, she said he was obsessed and he said yes with you. She said why don't you go to Europe and be a whore and a thief instead of trying to merge with me? I can't he said. Why not? she asked. He said she just said why and she knew anyway, he was tired of talking, and told her to take off her clothes before he took them off and she said nothing.

There's one condition, she said. His eyes bulged. He said name it. Don't hurt me, she said. Never, he said, but I'm going to be rough. She stood up, took off her suit jacket, folded it over the back of a chair, unbuttoned her silk shirt and did the same. She took off her brassiere that she wore only to work and he rose, and with one hand took her shoulder bare and round and with his other hand touched her breasts. His hands were busy. Hers were free. She stuck her thumbnail in his eye, he lept away and she raked his cheek, four gashes. Blood. He fell back on the sofa. She crossed to the fireplace, picked up the poker, returned and stood above him, gripping the weapon. She said she had come a long way, from faraway places where she'd learned certain things. He began to whimper. She raised the poker. He cringed. She swung. He screamed. The poker stopped an inch from his temple. She held it while he screamed. She touched his temple. He fainted. She threw ice in his face. He came to in blood, tears and icewater. Just one word. One word, she said, and you're dead. Understand? He nodded. Said he'd never bother her again. She said good. Got dressed. He said he was blind in his eye. She said just for a while. She walked to the door, and left, no looking back.

"Ever hear from him?"

"This morning," I said. I opened my purse and took out the envelope. "It came, as you see, with no return name or address, in my morning mail at work."

I handed him the envelope. He asked if my secretary had opened it, and I said my secretary thought it might be personal.

The note read—

> I can only say I am sorry. I know
> you will never forgive me, although
> I hope one day you will.

156

(I didn't)

I was on vacation for six weeks,
and wanted to see a psychiatrist
before I wrote. I hope things are
going well, and that you have every
happiness. I destroyed the dossier
and the films.

(signature)

He folded the note into the envelope and returned it to me. He
watched while I tore it up, and put it in the ashtray.

"This is why you wanted to tell me, today," he said.

"Yes," I said. "Circle complete."

We looked at each other.

"Something came between us back there," I said. "I don't know what
it was, but it was cosmic, and — terrific."

He said it was true, and made a little yelp. We held hands across
the table. He said I was wonderful, and I agreed, although —

"I know what you mean but you don't. Wonderful? Look in the dictionary. It's synonymous with strange, and it's for sure I'm strange."

"Aye, my lassie. It takes one to know one."

"I'm pretty shaky too, so think I'll have another drink."

"Good," he said. "Want to wait a while before my version?"

"Just until I get my drink." I caught the waitress's eye, and lit a
cigarette. Bingo. On the first sip of the cold liquid my spirits revived.
What a monster I am.

Thank God for that monster, his eyes said.

"Talk," I admonished. "Cut the monkeyshines!"

He grinned.

I smiled.

"You get that note this morning, and last night I had a dream, or
fantasy. I don't know which and I don't know the difference, nor do
I know if I was awake or asleep, but it felt like a spell. Flowing, but
not in rhythm, or maybe in a different rhythm, or well, anyway maybe
I *imagined* it. I met a girl, and — "

"You raped her," I interrupted.

"Yes, yeah," he agreed, "thanks. But I don't know, I felt I — she was

157

as if all or—I had the essence of the girl or young woman I've *hated!* I know it's wrong, etc., but those chicks I used to see in the singles' places, the one-night stands with them, the way they manipulated my cock, the way I was willing to be used, the way they left the next morning leaving me with—me, there. I know, a lot of guys like sex like that, but not me. I like to get to know a body. Anyway—it's happened— you have something to do with it, you've changed me, we're together, and for some incomprehensible reason something erupted last night and I realized that's why they'd wanted to leave, so once and for all, it seemed, it happened! I let her have it, and afterwards no I'm getting it backwards. She'd spent the night with me. We made it, slept and I woke up, looked across the room realizing it was dawn, and I thought I saw her in the shadows across the room. She was getting dressed, and with her shoes in her hand she headed for the door, but I came out of bed like a cobra, grabbed her, dragged her back to bed, pulled up her skirt, tore down her panties, threw her I mean threw her body on the bed, she didn't fight because she wasn't sure what she wanted, she hated me, pissed off oh yes and as I began, she got interested— why not?—and when I came she'd come at least twice, her eyes were crossed, she couldn't talk and when she got out of bed she stumbled, fell down, got up, pulled on her panties, straightened her skirt, picked up her shoes and headed for the door. I got out of bed, dressed fast, followed her down the steps onto the street, caught her a cab, and as she got in I said if you want some more you know where I live. She looked out at me, wide-eyed, with parted lips and her face blank, pleading, 'Okay?' "

I put out my cigarette, and watched him. He held up his hands.

"Peace, my love, this isn't my doing. This comes from outer space. Details are the point, stay in character, honey, I was wearing denim cutoffs, my yellow sweatshirt, and sneakers. She had been wearing— she was a blonde, a slender blonde, slender in her early thirties thinking she was ten less acting a solid ten under that with an IQ not over sixty and an attention span as short as her nose. Chainsmoker. Know the type? Anyway her hair was long, an important detail, and when she took off her grey flannel skirt I saw a small gold ID bracelet around her right ankle. Okay so far?"

"So far," I said, eyes on him. I knew!

He knew I knew, therefore he laughed. I smiled. Oh I loved him, but my smile was thin, a little grim, and my eyes were level.

He winked and my blood raced. I said—

"On with it."

"Okay, listen — what a day this has been what a weird mood I'm in, after work today walking down here to meet you, I passed a girl who was looking in the display windows at Altman's, and she looked very familiar indeed, and as I passed close to her, just a couple of feet away, saw what you have already guessed, the girl in my dream, fantasy or imagination, but get this. The ID bracelet was around her *left* ankle, and she was wearing a yellow sweatshirt, denim cutoffs and sneakers, and her hair was short, and cut and combed in the same style as mine."

* * *

We walked home, arm in arm in thought. Many things to think about and much to say. Yes, so much to think of, yes so much to say. We had talked in the restaurant and we agreed a dream had come true. A dream, for a couple of lovers side by side sailing through space.
One two three, four five six, seven eight nine.

Many things have been left out of my story, but I'll remember them, in my hard way, for me. The reader needn't know, save that I was with him until he died in the light of uncounted moons, and in his sleep: I found him so, beside me, seven dawns back.
And in that event, I determined, I would bring the final circle to its most complete full round. I had met, some while ago, a woman with whom I became the closest of friends, and so it was she moved in with me, and is sharing this beautiful place overlooking the river.

I had kept Christmas card contact with my dearest Saviour, all along, and had, not long ago, read of his death in the papers. His wife had died before him, so too in tragedy — an airline disaster — had his son, leaving a single grandson who was married, and studying in medical school. Therefore, having kept apace with events, I did a little looking into things, and made up my mind, having known all along which the good reader may guess, I took out my blue satin cloth, un-folded it, and looked at my still burning gems, folded them back in again, put them in my pocket and took a cab to a certain district in the middle of town for my final dealing with the underworld — after

159

first getting too cautious estimates from retailers who wouldn't believe what their eyes told them—I made contact with a fence who gave me an offer I couldn't turn down. I had my small, matte black Star .28 in my purse in case of any mischief, and as the crook counted out the money, we watched each other in the way persons do in that sort of transaction. I put the cash in my purse, snapped it shut—cool, final, I opened the door, he asked,

"What's your name?"

"Madame Curie," said I. "Yours?"

"Pierre."

I smiled my little old lady's smile, we exchanged pretty eyes, and I left, caught a cab home and that evening telephoned my medical student. A child answered. I asked was Mommy or Daddy at home?

"Mommy, it's for you," and as if the child's mother had answered the phone herself, her voice appeared so fast, I introduced myself, and she listened to prepared diplomacy—calculated to arouse curiosity in a sense of friendship—it was thus arranged I could visit on the evening of the day after tomorrow. But I couldn't stay long, for he had his studies. I said that would be fine, as I wasn't able to stay long anyway—the pleasant occasion didn't require it, at which I could almost visualize her wonderment. We said goodbye, and I lowered the receiver with a smile.

Therefore, on the appointed evening my friend and I took a cab across town to the address, and to our delight there was a comfortable luncheonette on the corner, and as she read Browning, I left her happy indeed in a booth by herself, drinking a cup of cocoa.

I went around the corner, was buzzed into the building, took the elevator to the designated floor, walked down the hall and touched the bell, which made a distant burr, and a moment later the door opened and I was facing a young, disheveled, dishwater blonde woman with grey eyes, no makeup noticeable and a boy and girl, each around four or five, standing close on each side of her. Six eyes, of much the same color, were fixed on mine as I said hello and went inside. She closed the door, offered to take my coat but I said no, I'd be leaving soon, so she indicated a chair next to a sofa across the room, to which I went, as she turned down the tv asking me if I wanted anything—a cup of coffee, or tea? Tea it was. With honey. I had or was being informed from the kitchen that her husband was washing up and would be in soon, so while I waited, with my purse in my lap, I looked around while the two children stood by the sofa looking at me.

The apartment was small, typical—the necessary kind—and in a nice

160

mess, the mess of life, with scents of milk, coffee, cigarettes, canned vegetable soup and urine, and as a memory, a woman's perfume. I talked with the children, got their names, they got mine, and Mommy appeared with a cup of tea in a saucer, and in the saucer a spoon. In her hand holding this, also a paper napkin, but with her other hand she removed a newspaper from a small table, put the table at my side, and the napkin and tea on the table and the newspaper on the floor with an apology. She sat on the sofa, I stirred my tea, and the children sat beside her in one motion, thumbs in mouths.

I remarked that the children were handsome, and had her eyes.

"Do you enjoy getting presents?" I asked her. "This is good tea."

"Lipton's," she said, and smiled yes, she loved getting presents, but I saw she was thinking.

"Good," I said, as her husband came into the room.

"Don't get up," he said, shaking my hand as we introduced ourselves. He cleared a wood and canvas chair of alphabet blocks and plastic toys, and sat down a few feet from me. We were facing each other.

He was a plain-faced, clean-shaven young man, with thin, light brown hair, and greenbrown eyes — both his and her bodies and hands were long and slender, yet in detail they were very different, but in stance, motion and outline, they looked alike. He seemed nervous, and was in truth more talkative. Typical of his profession, he led. And in the unhappy typicality of her role, she waited. Not that she was shy. He was the shy one. She seemed his confirmation. He said,

"I didn't know Granddad very well. He was away a lot. I liked him, he was good to me" — he glanced at his wife who nodded — "and to us, too, but as no one — well, nobody knew what he did for a living, or where he went on those overseas trips, the family suspected something shady, in an unspoken sense. He said he was a salesman but we never knew what he sold. It was all very technical, but after his son — my father — died, Mother cracked up and Granddad he disappeared for almost two years. Grandma was miserable without him — remember?"

His wife nodded. "Well," she said, "Grandma felt he — Granddad was closer to them than she was. Or she felt he was. She didn't say anything, but that's what I felt. She stayed in the background. But she didn't talk much anyway. Maybe I'm wrong."

"Nobody said anything," he said. "They were quiet people walking soft. They kept secrets. Odd, in a way."

"Victorian," she said.

He laughed.

I waited.

"When did you meet him?" he asked.

"And where?" she asked.

I'd thought often and in detail of this moment, so I told them truth to fit the need.

They were drawn to it but puzzled, getting more curious with each word, for it seemed to strike a chord in them, as what I said they almost seemed to know—who doesn't love a mystery? Their eyes brightened, and their children, sensing a unique suspense, watching parental reaction in silence, when they should have been crying for jealous attention. But in all honesty I was captured too. Even though I left out so much, in the telling of my tale after so long, it was fresh, and I was as interested—nay, fascinated as they, as I found myself leaning forward, speaking in a steady narrative of distant countries, cities, names and dates, often breaking into the languages, creating a steady authenticity, of a living document in their living room, as I concluded my story when my Angel had held my face in his hands, and said—

". . . in the eye of God . . . all that was, will yet be new."

I finished my tea, put cup and saucer on the napkin beside the spoon on the table, and looked at them.

Her head was lowered, hands clasped in her lap.

He stared over my head.

"So I returned," I said, "got a job, and began again. I had a new life to live, and I've lived it ever since."

We didn't speak. This was the turning point. I said,

"There is, however, a point to my being here,—I didn't come to tell a good story, although I admit—"

We laughed—all of us, and then I told them about the jewels. Not in fact how I'd gotten them, but as prepared, a brief synopsis, concluding—

"They were my emergency stash, and no matter what happened, they were there, but when it was clear the emergency was over, they turned into a hidden albatross, for instead of potential aid they became a positive reminder of a most unhappy past."

"Yes," he said. "I see—thank you for telling us about Granddad, as well as all the rest. You didn't have to."

"True," I said. "But I wanted to."

"I'm glad," she said.

"Me too," I agreed.

I opened my purse, took out the sealed blue envelope (within which the registered check), and handed it to him.

162

"Your task in life," I smiled, "will be to help others. May I give you this, so I may help you, and — " I paused. She said,

"Please don't explain."

He took the envelope, looked at it, and then at me. I said,

"It would embarrass me if you opened it while I'm here. Would you wait until I've gone?"

He looked at his wife. They nodded. He shook his head.

"I'm having difficulty believing this."

I stood up — they jumped up, quick, astonished at my abruptness, but I held up my hand.

"Well," I chuckled, "don't worry, you'll believe it! For sure!"

I put out my hand. He took it. We shook. He speechless. I gave his wife my hand, and she clasped it in hers.

"Must you leave?" she asked.

I nodded.

"Will you visit us again?" she asked.

"Will we see you again?" he asked.

I gazed into her eyes, and then into his. "I think not."

They looked at me. But it had to be. I said,

"I've come full circle, and with what's in that envelope, I can hope to have helped continue — " I gestured to them, and to their children — "who knows how many more?"

I walked to the door, and opened it, but turned to them. They stood, in tableau, looking at me. How I knew! oh how *incomprehensible* it was!

"Can't we do *anything?*" she pleaded.

"Endorse it," I said, "and put it in your bank."

I looked at the children, and saying their names, bade them farewell, and looking at their parents, who looked quite like their children, I said —

"Thank you,"

and stepped into the hallway closing the door behind me.

In a sudden fright that they might follow, to thank me in return, I walked as fast as I could to the elevator, but in a calm — of common sense (the sum would stun them) — I waited in peace until the elevator door slid open. I stepped in, the door slid shut and I descended, got out at the lobby, crossed it, walked outside and around the corner to the luncheonette. It was just beginning to get dark. I went in, and sat beside my friend, who greeted me, and moved over in the booth, eyes on mine, expectant.

"He took it," I said. She kissed my cheek, and I felt her tears.

163

"Here here," I said. "None of that."

She put the bookmark in Browning's poems, asking me if I wanted anything, some tea — ?

"No. Let's go home."

So that we did, and as the cab made its way across the city I gazed out my window, seeing very little, for I felt so good. I thought of many things. Yes, many things.

At home we took off our coats, hung them up in the closet, closed the door, and for a moment stood, two little old ladies, looking at each other.

"There must be something you'd like," she said, for in truth I was weary, and at low ebb, feeling . . . bone tired. I asked,

"Do we have any opium?"

We did, thank Goodness, — and ah, how it hit.

We sat on our sofa, flowers on the table before us, in our warm, warm room, looking out the window across the river. I saw the texture of this here over all that out there, as a transparent fluid heart alive, in memory

One man at an airport. Another beside me, asleep

> his head on his pillow
> his hair all awry
> the curve of his cheek
> so new to me

"You know dear," I said, as they smiled — "if a body doesn't realize itself — "

Impact. Far, far beyond.

" — the world's in for it indeed."

Music —

Atoms dance before my eyes.

You

AFTER VERY LITTLE SLEEP he woke in a dream of a novel: solid and soft as a distant gong, and he relaxed in the dark, listening.

The first paragraph was clear, and the second, as the narrative advanced onto the two voices, beckoned creation.

One said: Watch that third comma, you don't need it: the narrative advanced into, consider into, though we're aware you're weary of the inward advance. Those, were the days.

He did a mental delete of onto and into and inserted toward, got out of bed, put on a bathrobe, brewed a pot and poured a cup of coffee, added a spoonful of leftover vanilla ice cream, crossed the large room to his desk, snapped on the flex-lamp, sat down, rolled in a clean white sheet of paper, and on the reverse side, in the lower left margin, made a pencil dot to indicate page completion: discipline: sixteen spaces down — on this title page — indent eight, and after a pause, in caps the title: YOU: five spaces down, pause, he began the first paragraph.

Filled the page with words, using paragraphs to keep it spacious.

Next page: made the dot on the reverse lower left margin, bam bam bam three double spaces down from the upper right, at tab number 60 typed the title, and after four touches to the space bar, page number 2, swung left three double spaces down, and on margin tab 10 continued his narrative, with some worry, and as always, doubt: context not yet clear, yet it will be it must be, writing concern caused doubt of the experiment, he hadn't written anything that wasn't an experiment, was as disciplined to pause and think as he was to continue, a fact as fresh as tedious prose patterns tested by continuous enthusiasm: wit and image, the mind of the writer writing watching what was being written, hearing what will follow deleting with insertions along rewrites on the way to final composition, was, he judged, if even taken at face value, as interesting as the manuscript he was writing, which he wanted, in fact, the manuscript to be, and to be as good.

It seemed that writing or reading or doing neither — in his life he had

169

taken certain — things for granted, one of which was the story apart (dele) separate from the writer writing. All written work, he realized, and typed, in manuscript or in print, was written, — a puzzle left virgin in the full tomb of literature, but he had taken it for granted, well — wasn't that the way it was? regardless of the unwritten story how it not got written, and, this above all: the difference between.

As he typed he wondered if this was what writers were not meant to write. Writers. Writers! he knew the mirror of the page before him might be cause for an essay, but as lines of blue silk in Death Valley, he didn't want to write an essay, nor did he want to write about writers, not because writers were uninteresting, true, but because he was tired of thinking of writers in the way they were writers writing in that way because they were writers and no other, and he wanted to write a tale of a writer writing something not yet written about that.

In the last moon he had had an image that went round and round, and as it pleased him, he decided to use it at the beginning: a man and a woman walked along a sidewalk in a small, midwestern town. Late October.

"One of your standbys," the voice said.

"You you you again," said the other voice. "Keep writing, we can do it."

"Cut that comma. Insert a period."

"No. Keep writing."

The keys flew.

Breakfast is ready, she said, he wrote.

"No quotes?"

"No. He wrote that. We're not quoting what he wrote, we quote what he hears."

"And won't quote her?"

"We didn't hear her, it was understood he did. He hears us. Be still."

The voice was still, but, after a pause — "Yeah," it whispered, which went to show who was doing the talking in tough guy mysteries.

They crossed a leaf covered lawn, went up porch steps and knocked on the front door.

"That's you."

"Maybe," the writer said.

The door opened and a handsome woman dressed like a man said, "Come on in." She smiled. "Going to the game?"

"I don't know," the man on the porch said, wrote the writer, realizing they all had grey hair.

They entered and his wife closed the door. The man said, —
"We are three people with grey hair,"
can I get by with that?
"Sure, take them into the kitchen and give them coffee and — cookies.
Cake. Cookies. — Cake," the editing went so fast he didn't recognize
the voices, but knew he settled for cake because last night she had talked
about making coffeecake in the morning, and it had sounded good.

"Who's it about?"
Not cake. "Her son!"
"Don't write about *her*," the voice sneered. "*She* scared you!"
The writer made a mental note to make the woman in the house tall,
alluring, with grey eyes and platinum hair.

All this cover to make room for fiction, hearing a distant chuckle
as he realized he had thought in the nameless third person, a wander-
ing pronoun, wondering, along a parallel line if that was why so many
writers settled for nouns that sounded like pronouns, in the face of the
Ned Beaumont repeat, but writers were often hard of hearing, lazy,
and names were a fright.

They sat around the kitchen table, talking. Parents. The woman with
platinum hair seemed amused, in tension for Hugh. He'd broken his
arm last year, and this year sprained a finger in pre-season practice,
and here he was today, as eager as always, going in at quarterback
against the toughest team of all, Central High.

"That *is* you!" and the writer had the jitters typing:
"*You* again!" his wife hissed.
He said: "I'm not tough! I'm not from Central High!"
"You played against them!"
"Not with that name!" he barked at the keys.
"Look," her husband said: "we've come to visit — Jane. Can't you leave
that tone of voice—" he paused.
The writer paused.
"Back home?"
"Home? Where are you?"
"No, I meant he tells her to leave that voice, that tone of voice—"
"Back home. Well?"
He corrected the syntax.
The woman with platinum hair lowered grey eyes, stirred her cof-
fee, and spoke:
"Please."

171

Hugh came into the kitchen in uniform, helmet in hand, greeted the visitors, kissed his mom on the cheek, and as if (dele) dashed out of the house. An auto's engine roared into action, the player backed his machine into view—into the street, shifted gears, turned, sped out of sight.

"He's running late," she smiled. Grey eyes sparkled.

"What are the odds?" asked the man.

"On what?" he laughed. "On whom?" he typed.

"The game," he typed, baffled.

"Heavy against," murmured she with platinum hair.

The writer, dissatisfied with the color hair repeat, frowned, stared at the paper in his typewriter, and sat back.

"What next?" he asked. "Don't know," he answered, and fell into thought.

Stood up, pushed his chair back, walked into the kitchen and heated coffee, standing by the stove, thinking.

"Put 'em in a roadhouse and take 'em home."

"Not at the game?"

"The game!—I forgot!"

In the living room, he yet thought, remembering—God he hated that memory, and that drunken so-called father who sneered and mocked his son, while friends stood around embarrassed, the boy—*desperate* was the word, and that was the story he almost wrote.

But without knowing began a new novel, where the women kidnapped that highschool football star, and—of a sudden he was weary. He'd go over it later.

Took a nap, woke, had a cup of coffee, wrong, opened the refrigerator, took Stolichnaya from the freezer, filled two shot glasses, and went to the rear window, climbed out onto the fire escape where she was sewing. She looked up as he sat on a step and handed her the shot, which she accepted: they exchanged a glance, raised, and in a gesture, emptied the little glasses.

Good.

"How's it going?" she asked.

"I finished a story."

"What's it about?"

"I—" he began—hesitated. "I—I haven't read it."

"CORRECTION! *SAY IT!*"

"I—I—I—" panic: "I—*I don't know!*"

Printed January 1985 in Santa Barbara & Ann Arbor
for the Black Sparrow Press by Graham Mackintosh
& Edwards Brothers Inc. Design by Barbara Martin.
This edition is printed in paper wrappers; there
are 300 cloth trade copies; 200 hardcover copies
have been numbered & signed by the author; & 26
lettered copies are handbound in boards by Earle
Gray each signed & with an original drawing by
Fielding Dawson.

More than any other writer I can think of, Dawson strikes me as a writer who wants to locate and raise up into consciousness those rare, exhilarating moments that look in two directions at once . . . he's not after a Joycean epiphany so much as a moment which, recounted, creates both what preceded that moment and what must follow from it . . . he wants to recreate *all* of history, forwards *and* backwards. Thus his obsessive return to the act of remembering, instead of to the memory itself. This is risky business: we may get a narcissistic portrait of the rememberer, as indeed we sometimes do. We may get simple sentimentality, which now and then, we do. Or, as is more frequently the case, we may be let into a huge imaginative act that makes our own imaginations more truly, powerfully available to us.

— Russell Banks

Photo: Gerard Malanga

Fielding Dawson was born in New York in 1930, and, like many families during the Depression, moved according to his father's chances for work. Key West, circa 1935, with his sister Cara hunting seashells for a woman writing a book on same, thus, in author acknowledgement, his name, and his sister's, first appear in book form.

He grew up in Kirkwood, Missouri, went to Black Mountain College, served as a cook in the Army in Germany, returned, moved to New York in 1956, where he lives. He is also an artist, and in 1983 was the recipient of a grant, to paint, from the Adolph and Esther Gottlieb Foundation.